Cold Case 369

Cold Case 369

David Osborn

Published by Dagmar Miura
Los Angeles
www.dagmarmiura.com

Cold Case 369

First published 2022

ISBN: 978-1-956744-62-0

To Robin and Raphaella, with special thanks to my son, Sebastian, for his help in editing

One

It was mid-August and in the city of Covington, it was unbearably hot. The temperature, in fact, was only ten degrees Fahrenheit less in number than Covington's population of one hundred and eight thousand.

This was duly noted on the outdoor thermometer on the Roswell-Prentiss Pharmacy, which was located behind the blue-and-white-striped awning young Mr. Roswell had lowered early that morning immediately on coming to work. The thermometer was on the wall halfway between the front door and the double window to the door's left, where an oval shaped neon sign announced, unnecessarily, that the pharmacy was open, because it was already eleven a.m.

Putting down the newspaper rack he'd brought

out and casting a casual look across the busy street at the old town hall which some years before had become a near useless annex, young Roswell grimaced slightly before going back inside the pharmacy. He'd had enough noise and racket the past month from the annex being demolished.

Testifying to that, the two-century-old building was covered with a web of scaffolding that rose up the face of its three-story Victorian height and that failed to silence the occasional burst of jackhammers or keep within the thick clouds of brick dust that burst through its shattered windows. Two large dumpsters on the street outside further testified to the ongoing demolition where the town's citizenry had once lined up for motor vehicle registration and marriage licenses, or to seek document notarization.

Almost as soon as young Roswell had disappeared back inside the pharmacy, a workman appeared pushing a large loaded wheelbarrow into the gap caused by the total removal of a floor-to-ceiling second-story window. He tipped the barrow forward so that it tumbled a load of mostly broken old bricks into the dumpster directly below. A racket of debris falling into the dumpster's steel casing instantly ensued, along with a cloud of dust billowing out over the street.

The workman's name was Alberto Antonio, and he was an employee of the Saul A. Cort construction company contracted for the demolition. About twenty-five, he was slender and short in stature but a man whose long ropy muscles indicated a life of impoverishment and labor begun at a very young age. Clad only in a sleeveless undershirt, well-worn work-stained trousers, and heavy laced-up working boots, he used a moment's rest to gather his breath and wipe sweat from his face and neck with a dirty rag he kept tied around his head.

That done, he turned the wheelbarrow around and made his way with it some distance across the debris-scattered floor of the old building, where demolished lath-and-plaster walls had formerly separated various rooms.

Reaching the thick-walled brick remains of what had once been a city safe-deposit vault, he joined Jakub Walenski in prying loose from the surrounding brick one of a dozen of the once vault's steel safe deposit boxes still embedded in protectively thick brick walls. All, save for a few never used, had long ago been emptied and now hung half pulled out and void of contents.

Older than Antonio, Walenski was wearing a torn T-shirt emblazoned with the letters ATLANTIC CITY over a barrel chest where thick black hair, like the hair on his head, was matted with cement and brick dust. Without looking at Antonio when he came back and began to refill the wheelbarrow with debris, Walenski, his English accent thick, said bitterly, "What the fuck they want these goddamned things for?"

"To brick them up in a new vault," his fellow laborer offered, loading a heavy shovel full of debris into the wheelbarrow.

"Yeah, and like save some asshole big shot five bucks," Walenski growled. "Like they was broke or something and couldn't buy new ones?"

There was a heavy metallic crash as the box Walenski had been working around suddenly came loose and crashed to the floor in a shower of bricks. "Yeah, and fuck you too," Walenski said. He picked up the box and put it on a stack of deposit boxes already liberated from brick, then immediately began getting loose a new one that had never been opened. And muttering angrily as he did, "Bastards."

His fellow worker laughed. He didn't give a flying shit about the deposit boxes. He was getting paid. That's all he cared about, his Friday night check. He was getting enough every week to pay his room rental in the flophouse, feed himself, and still send half his money back to his family in Nicaragua.

Both men labored in silence, and the young Latino was about to take yet another full wheelbarrow of debris to tip into the dumpster down in the street below when Walenski broke a silence with a surprised "Fuck!"

It was loud enough to be heard, and Alberto Antonio turned to see the burly Walenski kneeling on the floor over the safe deposit box he had busted open, and muttering again, "What the fuck?"

The younger man put down the wheelbarrow and went to look at the deposit box. It had never been emptied, and what he saw was what seemed to be official looking papers with stamps on them of some sort. *Someone had screwed up but good, that was for sure,* the young laborer thought. *The deposit boxes were supposed to be empty.*

"I'd better tell Whitey," he said. Whitey was Whitefield, the foreman on the demolition job. "Might be important." In the back of Alberto Antonio's mind was the thought that if the papers were indeed important, he and Walenski might get blamed for their not immediately reporting them.

"Yeah, maybe," Walenski muttered. His eye had caught something, and lifting back the top papers, he saw beneath them what looked like a piece of dirty old canvas laid out flat on the papers beneath it. "And hey. Look at this. Some old canvas."

But his co-laborer had already gone to fetch the foreman and was headed across the floor for the nearest ladder to the stair below, trying to remember where he'd seen the man. The floor below turned out empty save for a small group of workmen ripping up flooring at one end. He accosted one. "Seen Whitey?"

"Nah. Floor below probably. Or maybe the street."

In the basement, where a gang was winching the building's big boiler up a ramp, it was the same story. The foreman? Who knew? It was outside the old annex when Alberto Antonio finally found the man coming back from the 7-Eleven down at the corner with a bagel and a can of Pepsi. He approached him nervously. "Mr. Whitefield?"

"Yeah?" In his late fifties, Whitefield was a tall prematurely gray and balding man who in spite of the heat was neatly dressed, with a white shirt under a light windbreaker that had gold letters on it that said SAUL A. CORT, CONSTRUCTION.

"Mister, Walenski wants you upstairs." Alberto Antonio had already decided it was safest to leave himself out of the unwanted discovery of the deposit box. "The vault we're taking down. Walenski found something maybe important."

Annoyed at the interruption, Whitefield said, "Oh, Christ. Okay." But when he and the young laborer reached the second floor where the Latino had been working with Walenski, five minutes had gone by and Walenski was nowhere to be seen, nor was the deposit box, along with its contents.

It took some time before the foreman finally understood the stammered explanation from the surprised young Latino laborer as to what Walenski had pried loose from the wall of bricks that had once been a secure vault. Before he was half finished, the foreman quickly decided he'd better cover himself if it showed up someday that the papers the young laborer said were in the box were important.

He told Alberto Antonio to keep on working and then went downstairs and outside the half demolished building to where a traffic cop was guiding the occasional car or bus around a cordoned off part of the street, just beyond the pharmacy, where the street was occupied by construction equipment.

"Workers upstairs taking down a vault full of deposit boxes," he said. "Found something I think your guys might want to know about."

An hour later a uniformed cop accompanied by a plainclothes detective pulled up in a squad car, and the two men went upstairs to where the vault was being demolished. It was decided that a theft had been committed, and a thoroughly frightened Alberto Antonio was taken to the nearest precinct station, where he was duly interrogated by skeptical detectives. What had he seen? *Nothing,* he insisted. *Just some official looking papers.* Was he sure the papers had stamps on them? And most of all, where was Walenski? Did he and Walenski have a plan to steal the safe deposit box together?

It went on and on until the detectives decided Antonio was clean and gave it up. Walenski was the same story. Of his whereabouts, of where he'd gone with the deposit box, detectives again drew a blank. An attempt to find him through the labor exchange took time, as did a search of two city flophouses, one of which disclosed he'd stayed there a week but was long gone.

In the following month, it was found that the deposit box had been registered in the name of J. J. Reynolds, a finance company, with key rights assigned to an employee named Bernard Feist. The box had been opened just once, and three years before. But Feist, the only person who could possibly have helped detectives understand why the box had been left in the vault with its contents not removed, had died that spring of a heart attack.

Records of the J. J. Reynolds Company showed that the papers in the box were unimportant documents pertaining to a many-years-old land-grab scandal long since settled. There was no mention in their records of anything else in the box.

Reaching dead ends everywhere, any further investigation ceased. The case was perhaps erroneously noted even to be a case at all since its contents as well as the deposit box itself had been deemed worthless. The file on it was nevertheless numbered and filed away with other cold cases in the police archives.

Two

Seven years later the world had changed and along with it the city of Covington, which had added several thousand to its population. Young Roswell of the Roswell-Prentiss Pharmacy was no longer as young and had clearly put on weight. When he set down the wire newspaper stand under the awning over the pharmacy front door, he hardly glanced across the street where the demolition of the old annex building had so often annoyed him. In its place there was now a large and modern boxlike sixteen-story building of green glass. Surrounded by a well-trimmed lawn edged with flower beds, it was fronted by a neatly line-spaced parking lot where one saw the mostly high-priced cars belonging to the equally high-priced law firms and medical offices the building housed.

Covington's police force was different too. It had expanded to over a hundred and twenty officers, eight detectives of which were specifically attached, in two teams of four each, to the precinct's two Criminal Investigation Departments or CIDs. Monitors and desktop PCs throughout the two departments were connected to COMSTAT, or Computer Comparison Statistics, as well as to the FBI database. They had long ago replaced typewriters on every detective's desk and were backed up by a recently installed computerized forensic pathology and identity system by which a homicide victim's long decomposed features could be brought to living full-size on a screen from a skull barren of identifiable flesh.

Full forensic reports as well as pathology results could be flashed before any detective's eyes in a split second, which, along with a suspect's entire criminal record, instantly provided investigators with whatever information needed in an ongoing case.

And if the department's physical equipment had changed, many of the methods used by investigative officers had also. Nearly all relied less on intuition, hunches, or experience and more on statistics.

One such detective who had never changed, however, one who for the most part spurned modern technology, relying instead on step-by-step logical deduction, was a woman in one of the detective units of the CID in the second precinct. She was Detective Inspector Roberta Jones, or RJ, as everyone had always called her, since she flatly refused to recognize Roberta.

Only eighteen months from retirement, she was a tall, lanky, rather plain-faced woman showing brow wrinkles and crows' feet around blandly tired eyes and one whom some irreverent younger officers in the patrol division called "old horse-face." Devoid of any makeup and with straight dark hair streaked with gray, which she wore neck-length, her inconspicuous bosom, bony wrists, and long hands complimented all the rest of her.

She'd been a cop for close to forty years, ten of which had been spent in uniform. Few, if any, knew anything of her personal life other than that she'd been raised by a series of social services–appointed foster parents and had once been a professional boxer.

Brief in speech, she had no use for sloppy or rambling thinking, and although in no way unpopular with her fellow workers in the CID, she kept to herself most of the time. Intensely private, she never spoke of family. It was occasionally rumored, with cynics reasonably doubting it, that she was married, and always with the thought, *God help the poor devil if he exists.*

RJ was hunched over her desk in the CID office, dressed in her usual, which was a well-worn and badly tailored jacket hiding her police utility belt and with a blue workshirt tucked into pants vaguely matching the jacket. She was taking a break from the small windowless interrogation

room a floor below the offices and barren of anything except a table and two chairs facing each
other across it.

She'd been interviewing a witness to a burglary
she thought might even have been involved in the
crime. Her Glock 22, along with the taser, handcuffs, and phone she'd taken from her utility belt,
lay in a pile on her desk, which was also littered
with files. RJ always dumped her "junk," as she
called the standard police equipment that many
detectives left behind on an interview. "Tends to
intimidate people so they don't loosen up," she said.

She hadn't been there for three minutes and
had just opened a can of Pepsi when she was
summoned to see Lieutenant Haley, who was the
man in charge of her four-man detective unit. He
appeared suddenly by her desk and spoke only one
word. "Office."

It was a summons. RJ didn't like the disrup-
tion and muttered, "Oh, shit. What the fuck now?"
She had never given up the coarse language of the
boxing ring. Reluctantly, she pushed away from
her desk and sauntered into the lieutenant's private
office, which had a bookcase, its shelves stacked
with files, and a large desk with a comfortable chair.

"RJ …" Haley began when she'd shut the door
and the noise of the office behind her. "Have a
seat." Overweight, with a rapidly developing beer
gut, and in his fifties, with a rather weak chin and
occasionally watery eyes, he was a veteran cop himself, and he followed with what he always said when

about to exert his status by lecturing or disciplining one of his detectives in a his usual no-excuses manner. "How's the witness thing going?"

"Lying his head off," RJ said, and thought, *What's next? He didn't ask me in about the bloody witness.* She didn't like Haley. She thought him weak and really unfit for the job, and she had a firm conviction of his being a willing puppet of Bruce O'Connor, the police chief of their precinct to whom he was so often seen sucking up to, or so surrendering to as to seem to have no mind of his own.

It took only a brief moment to find out. Haley muttered, "Okay. Stick with it," off-handedly. Coming out of a protective slouch, he put on defensive aggression. He said, "You've been without a partner now for how long?"

She didn't answer. It had been four months since her partner of many years, a detective in his fifties with a wife and three teenage daughters, had been shot through the gut when answering a domestic violence call. She'd tried but had failed to stop him from bleeding out before the medics came.

"Four months," Haley said, answering for her. "So you're getting one. Young woman name of Calibresi who made sergeant stripes when in uniform. She's fresh out of school, but she gets top-drawer references."

Everything in RJ froze. The last thing in the world she needed or wanted was another partner, especially a rookie. "Like what?" she said.

Haley was prepared. "Like the College of Criminal Justice in New York, the police academy, and six months in state detective school." He'd done none of that himself but liked to pretend he had.

"I don't need a partner," RJ said.

"She'll be in tomorrow." Ignoring RJ's negative was Haley's way of ordering. He said dismissively, "See she has a desk set up near yours. Show her the ropes. Help her get acquainted."

RJ silently rose and walked out of his office, firmly closing the door behind her. She'd sworn to herself when her partner had died to never work again with another person. But there was no point in arguing with Haley or trying to make a case. In her view he was too stupid or too narrow to understand what partnerships meant to detectives. Working together, sometimes under extremely dangerous circumstances, they often became so close as to be able to read each other's minds.

Back at her own desk, she took a long swig from the opened Pepsi can, put it down gently, and after staring at it a moment, said quietly, "Shit," and then, "Shit, shit, shit."

She finished the Pepsi, rose, and headed back to the interview room, which could be looked down on through a one-way window as well as on a special computer monitor. She was going to get the son of a bitch awaiting her to spill it if she had to keep him at the table for the next forty-eight hours.

Three

In a small third-floor studio apartment in a quiet residential block in a fringe area of Covington, Gina Calibresi awoke hating herself. Her name wasn't really Gina, it was Giulia, but nobody when she was a kid could handle that, and they'd called her Gina, and it stuck. Her head pounded with hangover, her body felt tortured from spent passion with the guy.

But it wasn't just the excessive drinking nor the sex that was so upsetting. It was because she had gone and broken every rule she'd firmly adhered to the past four years of what was basically training for the rest of her work life. And for being out of line yesterday, of all days, when she should have been watching the box with nothing more lethal to drink than a soda. Or, better still, playing her rather old and undistinguished violin, which she did well enough to have several times filled in for someone sick in the violin section of a philharmonic orchestra.

Rising after a painful struggle, she checked her bedside digital clock. Its red numbers said it was 6:20. Head throbbing, Gina dimly realized she'd only slept about four hours and didn't dare sleep any further. Today was her first day on the job as a detective with the criminal investigative unit, or CID, and Lieutenant Haley had been specific about being on time. "I'm teaming you up with a vet, Gina, a gal we all call RJ. Her full name is Roberta Jones but nobody calls her that, and she's somebody you can learn a great deal from. She's been a detective for many years and is retiring before too long. So start right. She's a stickler for punctuality."

Gina staggered the short bare-floor distance to the kitchenette counter beneath the window of her little studio apartment to make coffee before she fully realized she was alone. The guy she'd picked up at the bar yesterday evening had gone. There was no sign of him, only the mess they had made of her bed, and memory slowly returned of drink after drink and throwing all caution aside and bringing him home. She could only remember him as being as irresistible as her own need.

A cold shower helped, washing the olive complexion of her Italian face and body, and then more coffee and a couple of Tylenol. Getting dressed after blow-drying her long dark hair and tying it into a ponytail she tucked out the back of a baseball cap, she tried not to succumb to the nagging guilt she felt at breaking her own self-imposed rules. Barely conscious she was doing it, she hummed some of the lyrics to an old Cole Porter song, "It was just one of those nights / Just one of those crazy flights / A trip to the moon on gossamer wings / Just one of those things ..."

At twenty-eight, Gina Calibresi wasn't at all prone to one-night stands. It wasn't that she was an overly cautious woman, or a prude, or had been trained into suppressing healthy desire by priests or parents or anybody else. With her it was simply that there was a time and place for romance, if you could mistakenly call last night's impetuosity such. It meant putting passing feelings on a back burner and not letting them interfere with her life, which for the past several years meant first things first and getting up the ranks of a police force from constable to sergeant, then finally detective.

Yesterday, dressed in what she had laid out as appropriate for today, pants and a shirt and jacket, but without police regalia at her waist, she'd foolishly decided she needed a pre-celebratory drink, perched on a bar stool. It had been a relief not to be putting on the uniform she'd worn for three years as an officer with a car unit.

But forget last night, she urged herself, returning to normalcy when she pinned her badge to her waist and strapped on, out of sight under her jacket, a handgun holster with a Glock 22, handcuffs, phone, and taser. She was a cop, better still a detective, and proud of it. She'd paid her dues in the lower ranks.

Another glance at her bedside digital. 7:25. She was to report at 0800. So she was right on schedule. *Okay, all right, then, let's go,* Gina thought. Grabbing car keys from her dresser, the only furniture in the room besides the bed, she paused briefly to glance at four small framed photos also atop the dresser. They were her life, past and present, and she said good-bye to them every day when she went to work. It was ritual.

One photo was of herself not in police uniform but seated in the violin section of a philharmonic orchestra playing a violin and looking up toward a conductor. The violin she sometimes used on one of those rare occasions stood mostly abandoned in its case in a corner near her bed.

The photo next to that one was of a clearly Italian couple in their twenties, a third was of a young Air Force fighter pilot standing by his big lethal jet. Glancing at it, Gina's eyes narrowed in anger and she said, "Bastard. I hope you fucking spin in or something," and then softened before reluctantly leaving the photo.

She had been all the way in love with the pilot and engaged to marry him when it had come to a sudden and completely unexpected end the night when, instead of getting ready for bed after dinner and wine to celebrate her promotion to sergeant, he'd abruptly announced, "I'm sorry, Gina, but there's somebody else. I have to call us off." Two years later, she was still in love with him. She couldn't help it.

The fourth photo was of an older man and his wife, which she briefly picked up to brush with a kiss. "Wish me luck, you two," she whispered before she left her apartment, firmly locking its door behind her.

The picture of the older couple was of George and Flora Shaw, whom she adored, the ones who had bestowed the nickname of Gina on her, and whom she'd always called Mom and Dad, and who had adopted her soon after she'd been placed with them by social services. Her real parents, the young couple in the other photo, had died in a plane crash in which she herself, barely three years old, had been one of the few survivors.

She had seen George Shaw, especially, a kindly and loving police detective, as an icon all through her growing-up years before and during her teens and right through college as well, always putting her first before anything or anybody, including himself, and insisting, along with Flora, that she keep the name of her parents as it was on her birth certificate. "They were good people who loved you, Gina. Be proud of them and your Italian heritage."

George Shaw had finally given up on life soon after Flora had also gone but not until Gina was in her last year at the college they had picked for her and paid for.

It was because of George Shaw and as Gina

Calibresi that in her deep trust of him, she had given up music, urged to do so by him when he said, "Sure, music's okay, Gina, love, but you gotta have a career in something steady, know what I mean? Like mine in police work. Where there's a pension and sick benefits and all that. Music's gotta be something what you do on the side."

Still barely out of her teens, she had reluctantly yielded to what she thought, loving him as she did, was his far superior wisdom, built on a lifetime of worldly experience, and with a heavy heart had mostly abandoned music. Except for the occasional nostalgic foray to a chair in the violin section of one symphony orchestra or another, she had dedicated herself to police work and had learned to love it. After college, she had done courses at the John Jay College of Criminal Justice in New York, then while still a uniformed patrol officer, had gone nights to detective school.

Driving her old Volkswagen to her first job as a detective with the CID of the second precinct, she was excited. Always consumed by curiosity, she'd found detective work rewarding and could hardly wait to get started. She knew detectives were usually paired and hoped she'd be linked to a good partner and that the tech bunch backing them up would be compatible as well as competent.

It was a short trip in time since rush-hour traffic hadn't yet started to build up, and she was soon at the police station, where she found a place to park with other ordinary vehicles beyond a line of police cars before entering the police department through a door directly under a sign saying POLICE.

She found the ground floor just as she'd seen it the day before when meeting with Lieutenant Haley, an all but too familiar lobby with groups of uniformed officers coming off or coming on duty, with a desk sergeant interviewing someone and several people awaiting their turn to talk to him.

She paused the briefest moment, remembering her own part in the same first morning bustle in another city she'd worked in for three years. Then she took a breath and went upstairs to the CID to which she'd been officially attached and where she would be regarded once again as a rookie, the way she had been when first out of police school and assigned to uniform patrol.

She found the office surprisingly quiet. Of the dozen or so desks, only a few were occupied. PC monitors rising up over stacked papers, scattered pens and pencils, telephones, and various office paraphernalia, were dark. Other office equipment was silent. The door to the lieutenant's office was open and the office unoccupied. A wall clock said it was 7:50. She was ten minutes early.

She felt relieved but also awkward and very much new there, and she was standing near the Lieutenant's open door wondering what to do next when she was accosted by a young man in shirt-sleeves, carrying a load of files and a coffee. He wore large horn-rimmed glasses and said abruptly, "You're who?"

Gina introduced herself and added, "I was told I had a desk some place."

"Ah, yes," the young man said. "Charlie Fargo. Data research. I think your desk is over there with the other detectives and someplace near RJ, so good luck." A short meaningful laugh followed with a cautious point with his coffee cup hand and he was gone, plunking down at a desk where she recognized the computer system used in the data analysis of crime.

Gina headed in the direction he'd pointed to, and wondering where he'd got the coffee from, kicked herself for not asking him. Others she would soon meet had started coming in behind her. The office nerd, Ace DeSalles, a forensic pathology expert attached to the unit; Roy Cohen, who monitored the ATF and FBI data channels; and Alice Detroit, an older all-purpose motherly secretary, who had achieved a seniority role but was everyone's dogsbody.

Alice possessively ran the coffee machine and, as she was offering Gina one, a hurrying Megan Adler rushed by, and without stopping, threw a "Hi, welcome aboard. Talk later."

Megan, known to all as just Mimi, was partnered as a principal detective with Pete Zoraan, who'd given up professional hockey for police work. Gina was to learn that Pete had been shot in a bodega holdup and saved with CPR by Mimi, and that he and Mimi were inseparable.

There were others, like Perkins, the civilian

office boy, and Randy Scott, an intern. The office, when busy, was often an insistent mix of sound, of people talking and telephones ringing, and had the intimate air of a closed club, a group of people living in their own world.

Gina had no trouble finding her assigned desk. It stood glaringly swept clean save for a little name plate stand that said only CALIBRESI, which was dwarfed by a neatly stacked pile of files. The desk was surprisingly close to another one, already occupied by a tall, thin, getting-gray woman in a rather too old jacket who sat at it, peering intently at her monitor.

"Gina said, "Hi."

There was no response. At her own desk, and not knowing quite was expected from her, she realized the files must have been placed there for her to look at, if not there accidentally. She pulled down the top one and opened it. She'd hardly done so when the graying older woman, without taking her eyes off her monitor, said, "When you get through that lot, there are more where they came from."

Gina said, "Are they closed or active cases?" She waited out a long silence, then heard, "Cold." The tone was disinterested.

"I take it I'm assigned to them," Gina said.

There was no answer, and Gina's short fuse lit. She might be a rookie, but this lack of response her first moment there was rude dismissal. She rose and went to stand directly opposite the woman, across the desk. "You must be RJ," she said with as much smile as she could muster. "I'm Gina Calibresi, your new partner."

And when the woman, without a word, slowly and after a long silent moment raised her eyes from the monitor, she added, "Oh, good. You are RJ, right? I'd hope so. I thought from your silence I'd got the wrong person, or you were maybe avoiding me."

She waited. She'd meant her comment as a joke. Had she badly overstepped? This was someone she was assigned to work with, like it or not. It seemed forever before the reply came.

"I didn't ask for you. But as long as you are here, get to work on the backlog of cold cases that neither I nor any of the other detectives have had time for, but which have to be reviewed and cleared, if possible. Return the ones on your desk to Records, and note any still down there that should be reinvestigated."

With that, RJ returned her attention to her monitor and began typing an email, and Gina, badly taken aback and painfully disappointed, realized she'd lost battle one with the woman with whom she was to partner.

Retreat gracefully, she said to herself, realizing even as she thought it that studying the CID's cold cases would indeed be a good way to start her job. If she was careful not to make any embarrassing mistakes, she'd learn a lot.

She had no idea how much.

Four

The archives or records of the CID, along with all the rest of the second precinct police department, had been long relegated to a windowless basement room in which a near perpetual dead silence dominated a wall of large file cases that in turn were almost dwarfed in importance by several rows of floor-to-ceiling records jammed close together onto steel shelving like the crowded stacks of a library. Each aisle was lit by a solitary unshaded light bulb hanging down from the ceiling.

All this was presided over by the figure of Helen Rothstein, irreverently called "the troll" by upstairs officers. A civilian employee of the city, her nearly forty years of experience had soured her on life. Except for her regular weekly bridge club attendance, she had little use for anybody, and her evenings in her small apartment were invariably spent looking at Netflix romance streamers. She was seen constantly bent over a magazine spread out on the nearly swept-clean surface of a desk lit by only one LED light. Long divorced as well as alienated from her one child, a married daughter, her overly full bosom complemented a prematurely aging face, topped by the bluish tint of a rigid perm.

Helen lived in a world of her own and had as much disdain for the officers of the detective unit, the members of which were most of her visitors, as one and all they had learned to have for her. She lived by the old edict, "Heaven helps those who help themselves," and whatever the problem, nearly always found a way not to leave her desk and help a questioning detective find the right file he or she needed to examine. She had learned over the years that most were usually capable of solving any problem they had by themselves.

This was something Gina Calibresi found out the moment she entered the archives through the door at the foot of the stairs carrying the stack of files registering cold cases never solved and which had occurred in the past five to fifty years.

"Returning these," she said on reaching Rothstein's desk at the beginning of a first line of file shelving.

The archivist managed to look up from reading a popular woman's magazine to give a deceptively warm smile.

"You're new," she said, seeing the stack of files. "File name or number?"

Gina glanced at the top file. It was marked only SERIAL CAR JACKING.

The archivist compared it favorably to an equivalent identification in her large black and long used ledger book. Then, looking back down at the magazine she'd been reading, she said, "Put them back where they belong, like a good girl, would you?"

"Okay", Gina replied, "but how do I know where that is?"

"Follow the markings." And the dour archivist turned a page of her magazine, still without looking up.

Gina figured it would be smart not to bother the woman further. She'd been warned by the data specialist, Charlie Fargo, that she'd find searching cold-case files difficult. She decided that the *A* before a number on one of the files meant the aisle it was on, and this proved right. From close by the desk of the archivist, each one of the stacks disappearing into the badly lit gloom was labeled. There were four, A, B, C and D, and she started down the A aisle, slowly looking for a box or boxes marked COLD CASES or just CC. There were floor-to-ceiling shelves, six in all, and on each shelf there was a box on which the identity of its contents of a particular crime or case had been clearly written.

Gina worked her way until, nearly at the aisle's end, she finally encountered a box clearly marked CC, that was the top one of a stack high on the shelves and was almost out of reach. After a struggle, she managed to pull it down and get it open, revealing that it mercifully held only a dozen or less files. Some were only marked by year while others were marked mysteriously by numbers that were in the three hundreds.

She put the case down on the floor, and kneeling beside it, discovered, in what light there was, that there was a total of eleven files. She took them out and replaced them with the ones RJ had piled on her desk, which she'd brought down, and then took all eleven back to Rothstein, whom she found still indulged in her magazine.

Hearing Gina coming, the archivist looked up barely long enough to notice Gina's armful and said, "Have to sign them out." Smiling as though winning a fight over something, she slid the worn ledger book toward Gina from where it was presiding across her desk. "The time and the date for each, Detective, and your signature where indicted."

Gina silently put the files down and one by one did as the older woman ordered. It took what seemed forever to find the dates on almost all of the eleven she'd brought. Papers in them were jumbled about and mixed up, and Gina had to rummage through each file in order to identify it.

Exasperated, she said, "Some of these files are numbered in the three hundreds. That's an impossible lot of cold cases. What happened to all the cases before these?"

Without looking up from her magazine, Rothstein said, "Numbers got mixed up with live cases ten years back. Up to three hundred something, they were all active."

Some filing system, Gina thought. It was with real relief that she finally left the silent and half-lit archives, saying nothing but a muttered "Thanks," to which there was no reply from the archivist, still too buried in her celebrity magazine to care.

Back in the upstairs office, now busy with ongoing police work and in sharp contrast to the morgue-like silence she'd endured in the room below, Gina was rewarded with only a slight glance from her newly appointed partner. RJ didn't bother to ask if she'd found what she was looking for, and without a word herself, Gina got busy and dug into the files.

Some were thick, indicating extensive investigating; some were surprisingly thin, showing little interest. They were filed according to date. Gina read them all, beginning with the most recent one, which contained the various detectives' admissions of failure to find any trace of a missing seven-year-old child believed abducted. One of three siblings of loving parents, she had happily gone to bed with her favorite Raggedy Ann doll and was kissed good-night by her parents. There'd been no sign of illicit entry into the house. All doors had been locked for the night by her father before he went to bed himself. Her two sisters had never woken.

An exhaustive two-year search produced not a single clue as to why or by whom the child had been taken. She'd gone to bed and then, in the morning, her bed was empty. It was as though she had simply disappeared into thin air.

The last file Gina studied was a homicide that had occurred twenty years previous. A woman real estate agent had been found dead in her car parked in the driveway to her suburban home at seven in the morning. She'd been shot in the head by a nine-millimeter handgun from some fifteen feet away, indicating the killer was outside the car and had fired through an open window. The gun, however, was never found, even though an autopsy extracted the bullet from her skull and a comparison was made between marks on the bullet with known marks in the barrels of the hundreds of possible guns used for the killing.

The FBI database of firearms used in previous criminal cases, as well as that of the ATF, was compared to police records. Fingerprints and DNA samples taken from the car proved to be her husband's, but it had been confirmed he'd been abroad on business at the time of her death. The file was thick with details of endless interviews and investigations of friends and neighbors. Three members of the CID had exhaustively pursued the case only to finally admit defeat and file their efforts away in the basement archives.

Altogether, Gina's efforts on the cold case files were unrewarding. There was nothing she hadn't already come up against in her work as a uniformed patrol officer or picked up in hearing after-work chatter from detectives. Or in cases lectured on or studied in detective school. So it was with little reluctance that she pushed back in her chair from her desk and prepared to call it a day.

It was late; the office had quieted. Most had quit for the day, her hostile partner among them. The files she's brought up were piled neatly on her desk to be returned tomorrow to the dour old archivist, their contents a blur. She'd learned nothing from them to get her started in the new job. Missing children, homicides, serial killings, armed robberies, corporate frauds, they all merged into one useless jumble of endlessly contradicting facts leading to failure to solve.

All except one marked A-369, which she found curious in its lack of questioning, something that to her was basic in any serious police work. Perhaps, she thought, it was because the theft involved was so unimportant in itself compared to scores of other far more serious cases that it wasn't seen worth anything but the most superficial investigation.

Some seven years ago, detectives had been alerted when a workman, demolishing part of an old annex to city hall, had apparently lugged off an unemptied safe deposit box that had spilled out of the bricked-up walls of an abandoned vault. The box was owned by J. J. Reynolds Ltd., an independent finance advisory group with key rights granted to one of the company's employees, a Bernard Feist.

The only witness, a worker named Alberto

Antonio, who had barely glimpsed the contents of the box, was considered unreliable. He'd said he thought the box contained papers, which company records revealed to be outdated and worthless copies of legal correspondence of no importance.

Detectives had accordingly decided that the worker who had stolen the deposit box, one Jakub Walenski, must have mistakenly, in his ignorance, seen the papers as possibly useful somehow. It was the only reasonable explanation for his theft.

Walenski, who had disappeared with the battered box, hadn't returned to the job, but given that both the box and its contents had been judged to have been of no value, there was little serious investigation as to where he might have gone beyond his having lived in a nearby flophouse. Nevertheless, a theft was a theft, whether thousands from a bank robbery, a chocolate bar from a grocery store, or a battered safe deposit box, and the worker's running off with the box had, at the time, been filed as a cold case.

On her way home to her tiny studio room in the suburban apartment block, Gina just the same kept wondering. If detectives had gone so far as to inquire about the contents of the box, why hadn't anyone also inquired about an assigned keyholder, one Bernard Feist? Besides his being an obviously trusted employee of the J. J. Reynolds company, who was he? And why had he been granted key rights? Other than his name, there was nothing about him at all. He'd been into the box only once and that was three years before its discovery during the demolition. Just once? That struck her as rather odd.

Fixing herself a drink before eating a prepared dinner she'd picked up on the way home from the local supermarket, Gina settled down alone to watch a favored streamer and kept thinking about it. No presumption had been made that perhaps, just perhaps, Feist might have opened the box that one time only in order to place something in it.

And that was the very reason, Gina thought, to at least investigate a little further. If she found out that there was indeed something in the box besides papers, and if it somehow had meaning or possibly even value, she would have cause to possibly revive the case and pursue it further. But where to start? With the worker whom the police had never found, the box owner, or the employee who had key rights? Possibly an impossible search, she thought, but worth a try, and if for no other reason than to satisfy her curiosity.

After work, loneliness set in, taking the place of any further thoughts about it. She fixed herself another drink and glanced at her violin and thought to play a piece from a Bach interlude, but then felt too tired to do so. Instead she collapsed on the bed and switched her iPad to a streamer, as she did trying not to remember that she'd shared her bed the night before with a guy she'd met in a bar, unexpectedly yielding to the desires of a man whose name she couldn't even remember. She was a detective with work to do and had no time or wish for that sort of untoward surrender to not wanting to be alone.

But thinking that didn't seem to help. Loneliness took over again with all its nagging hollow-shadowy pain. After an unbearable while, Gina stripped off for bed, then impulsively went to her dresser and took down the picture of her Air Force pilot. Getting under the covers, half crying, she held it close to her breasts and turned off her bedside light.

Five

About the time Gina Calibresi was out of college and beginning her career first as a uniformed patrol officer, and Roberta Jones, aka RJ, was well up the ladder to a major career as a Detective Inspector, Jakub Walenski had abruptly stopped the hard work of demolishing a heavily brick-walled office vault. Looking down through the still swirling dust of falling bricks at the safe deposit box that he had loosened from the wall and then had wrenched open with his wrecking bar, Walenski found himself wondering why things had been left in it.

The pack of papers that were in the box had official stamps on pages of type and were marked CONFIDENTIAL. That had to mean they were big-shot important. There were guys he'd heard who had a handle on how to sell things like them. Who knew if they could be worth something.

And what about the dirty old canvas hidden underneath them? He carefully turned it over and found himself looking at the dust and grime-smeared painting of what seemed to be an old woman wearing a bonnet and seated by a window reading a book.

What he saw jolted him. A painting? What the fuck. Why would anybody put a painting like that in a deposit box? Was it maybe worth something too? Deposit boxes were for storing valuable things in them so nobody could get at them, weren't they? Like money or important papers or jewelry.

Then, staring at the painting, and almost at once, thoughts began to jumble about in his head. Wait. Maybe take both it and the papers. There wasn't nobody there to see him do it. Yeah, sure. The Latino never got a real look. Hide both the fuckers somewhere and keep working like you'd never seen nothing that counted.

He looked around. There was no sight of Alberto Antonio or anybody else save for a couple of guys at the far end of the floor taking down what was left of a ceiling. *Fuck's taking forever,* he thought, wondering why the Latino was so long getting the foreman. And then, and almost without thinking, it flashed in his mind: *It was now or never.*

Walenski took the canvas from the deposit box and began to roughly shove it under his Atlantic City T-shirt. It didn't go easily, corners got caught in the sweat-matted hair of his body, the outline of the canvas clearly showed. The foreman would see and ask questions.

He tried quickly doing the same with the papers, stuffing them, also, first behind his T-shirt and then down into his pants. But they were too thick a packet, and it was the same as the canvas. They showed.

A new thought and everything in Walenski froze. All the noise of the demolition silenced: the piles of brick and debris around him, the dust still hanging in the air, all were unseen. He'd almost forgotten. The damned Latino was getting the boss to look at what came out of the bricks, wasn't he? That Whitey fuck? And Whitey could be there at any moment. A voice in his head said, *Wait. Suppose Whitey also thinks the canvas picture and the papers are worth something and grabs them? Don't take no chances. Maybe get both the hell out of here. And right now. It's coming up five o'clock quitting time in an hour. Tell Whitey tomorrow you quit early because you felt sick.*

He heard voices. Almost without thinking, he jammed papers and the canvas back into the deposit box to hide them, grabbed up the box, and ran for a back stair that took him out of sight in seconds.

Nobody saw him leave, going down with the box into the alley where they once had put filled-up big trash bins for the waste trucks that came early mornings. And nobody paid him any notice as he went along the street to the bus stop, trying not to be seen even when he finally got there.

All the while he had but one thought that made his heart race. It was to get away and get away fast to someplace safe where he wouldn't get caught. And it got even worse when he made it onto a bus with people giving him looks because of the sweat running down him through the cover of brick dust still all over him and with him still clutching the box. There'd been no time to get rid of it in one of the building's trash bins with some jerks working the basement coming into that alley to piss. Now he was glad he hadn't. Some nosy fuck on the bus would think it strange, his carrying papers and a painting, and ask questions. The box hid them.

And it was like that until he finally got off the bus and found a place to get rid of the box, dumping it into a city litter can he found empty. It didn't matter if he was seen doing it. He was in a neighborhood where nobody looked at anybody because they were all too busy just trying to survive. Many were homeless men with clothes in ruin who rarely showered or were cleanshaven and were listless and gaunt.

There was no one in the flophouse where he had a ten-bucks-a-week cot in one corner of an almost windowless second-floor room he shared with a dozen others, some workers, some drifters or alcoholics or into drugs. The air was heavy with the smell of unwashed bodies, urine, tobacco smoke, and alcohol.

With his back to the room to shield the papers and the grime-covered canvas, Walenski sat on his cot, which had two soiled blankets. One was to lie on and the other to cover himself with when he slept. He put the papers and canvas next to him and held up the canvas first to look once more at the painting of the old woman reading a book. A dark thought suddenly began to form. *Wait. When you think about it, maybe, who the hell would want some fucking old broad reading? Maybe the dumb painting wasn't worth nothing. Or maybe a buck or two only.*

But what about the papers, then? Walenski took a close second look, carefully noting the big official stamp of some kind at the top of each sheet and the word CONFIDENTIAL above a full page of print. Images of men in suits in some big office arguing over them again flashed through his mind. And once again he thought, *Somebody might pay good for these. Maybe a lot.*

The loud moaning wail of the siren on top of the firehouse a couple of blocks away interrupted his thoughts. It sounded off every day at five o'clock, and the one blast meant quitting time for workers all over. It reminded Walenski that they might be wondering at work why he wasn't there. This time, he succeeded in stuffing papers in his pants and the canvas under his shirt. Where he was, it didn't matter if it looked funny.

Then he left the flophouse and went to a fast food place for a burger, and when he'd finished eating, got a bag of chips and a Coke and took them to a run-down park nearby and sat on a bench, eating and thinking.

Chances of making some extra money from the deposit box loomed big, but he didn't want to throw his job under a bus. It was steady money. Maybe he'd go back in the morning, and if Whitey had something to say about why he'd quit early, maybe he wouldn't tell *Whitey* that his stomach had suddenly gone bad the way he'd thought, and that he'd had to run to one of the porta-pots lined up in the back alley for workers. And maybe not. Maybe instead he'd split town and look for another job elsewhere.

Sitting and thinking that way, Walenski decided also not to risk having the canvas and papers on him but to dump them quick. He'd figure somewhere next day. It had got dark, and finished eating, he went back to the flophouse and to his cot. He looked around. There were only a handful of guys the far end of the room. When he was certain they weren't looking, he got both the official papers and the canvas from his shirt and pants and shoved them under the blanket near where he lay his head. With a short laugh to himself, he found they made a good pillow, and pulled the other blanket up to his shoulders.

Settling, he had a last thought. What about that pawn shop, Billy's fucking Pawn or some name like that? He'd passed it a few times. Yeah, Billy's Pawn. Maybe if he stayed in town, he'd see what he might get there. A few bucks, maybe. Pawn guys bought things. Sleep finally overtook him.

Six

At some point on her drive home, the tall plain-faced middle-aged woman behind the wheel of the relatively new Honda stopped being RJ to everyone in the entire police department, where she had the reputation of being an almost legendary great detective. She'd been RJ too in the ruthlessly brutal women's boxing world, which had been her pre-cop past, as evidenced by the slightly pushed-in appearance of her nose and by the pulled-down outer corner of one eye, which still bore the scar of a fight-stopping punch.

When home, it was the only time she reverted to being Roberta, the name bestowed on her first by one pair of a half-dozen foster parents she'd suffered when she'd been dumped on them as a nameless thirteen-year-old orphan with virtually no identity. That was before she'd later found a life in the fight ring after finishing up a chaotic education in a string of different high schools, each one interrupted when she was moved to a different foster home.

Roberta Jones had no idea of her origins or even where she had been born. Most official evidence of her childhood had been lost in one bureaucratic fumble after another. After boxing, she'd used hard-earned money as a nightclub bouncer at a strip and pole-dancing club to cover her lost past with phony documents listing her name as Jones and gaining a place, first in police school, then as a rookie patrol officer with the Covington Police Department. She'd applied to the police because it seemed a secure job and because she'd always seen cops on top of things instead of at the bottom, a world she was all too familiar with.

Now, looking back at forty years of police work, she had finished one more day's duty, this time chasing down clues in a brutal murder that had occurred a week ago and which she suspected of being a serial kill, as she had found in the autopsy report a number of pointed similarities to a still unsolved murder that had occurred six months previous.

Cursing silently as the driver of another vehicle sharply cut her off, she braked hard and was nearly forced out of her lane and over the curb of the long tree-lined suburban avenue exiting town. Getting back into the light flow of traffic, she

tried to catch the offending car's license number—
the driver deserved at least a warning—but sight
of it was barred by another car he'd cut off, and
RJ's thoughts, recovered from the interruption,
returned to the case on hand.

It was like that with her. Any case virtually
became her life. To think of all the details of whatever work on hand was to immerse herself in it. If a
homicide, especially, she'd relentlessly dwell twenty-
four hours of the day on every aspect of the case
from the first view of the corpse and a thorough
inspection of the crime scene prior to Forensic taking over. She'd attend every aspect of the autopsy
and spend subsequent endless desk hours at her
computer analyzing clues and chasing down or
matching up data. And then, far too often, there
was the always sad business of notifying the relatives of the deceased, whether wife, husband, child,
elderly parents, or someone who was just a devoted
friend, while just the same using condolences as a
way to gather information.

RJ owned a small one-story house the real
estate people called a bungalow and which she had
bought three years ago, finally moving out of rental
when her carefully saved salary over the long years
of police work allowed her to buy and own instead
of endlessly bleeding what she earned into the
hands of some large corporate landlord.

The house was in a development of several
scores of similar houses. It had a one-car attached
garage and was separated from her neighbors only

by a low look-over fence and was set back from the street by a short car-length cement driveway just like theirs.

The day she'd moved in, RJ had taken a week off from work and occupied herself completely with planting flowers and bushes between the fence and the driveway. It helped her to separate herself from her neighbors, who on one side were a couple, the husband a retired rail engineer. On the other lived a still young pair, both of whom worked in some department of the government. RJ kept knowledge of her neighbors to a nodding acquaintance.

Driving into the garage and then entering the house by a door to the kitchen, she felt herself begin to relax. A stiff shot of ice cold whiskey lay ahead, along with a dinner that was a Dover sole, by the smell that pervaded the air, and then a quiet evening catching up on a TV show or just the news.

There was also the warm embracing love of Mireille, her partner of many years, who always would hear her driving up and coming in, and greet her arrival with a warm hug and kiss. Mireille was Mireille Chu, an Asian American who RJ had met when visiting in the city hospital an injured witness to an armed robbery she had been assigned to cover.

Mireille had been close by in the same ward. Once a pretty high school athlete and a softball champion, she had been blinded and her face badly acid-scarred in a vicious racist attack by two men who, as well as beating her with a chain, had knocked her to the ground, where for several minutes they had savagely struck and kicked her multiple times, leaving her unconscious, with a broken arm and ribs and a skull fracture.

RJ had got herself assigned to the case. Eventually tracking down the attackers, turning them over to the district attorney for prosecution for assault and attempted murder, as well as handing the case to the FBI for a hate crime, she had come into long contact with Mireille.

The young woman, her once pretty face ravaged by the scars left from acid burns, attended a school for the blind. And it was during that time that RJ not only fell totally in love with her but found her love reciprocated. Their *moment* had been when Mireille's fingers gently traced lines over RJ's face as she sought to know how she looked. When she'd taken her hand away, Mireille had said in a mock tone of wonderment, "Hey, you are just as lovely looking as me."

They both had laughed at the intimacy bringing them together.

"How was your day?" Mireille had already deftly set the dinner table for two along with a bottle of cold white wine and was poised to serve up the Dover sole. Her ability to move about when only seeing vague shadows from one eye, let alone to cook, to clean, and even to shop, continuously mystified RJ.

"Can you skip the whiskey?"

"For the sole you just cooked, I'd even skip recounting today's work."

Dover sole was RJ's favorite dish. She dumped her utility belt with its attached holstered gun, cuffs, taser, and phone, and they sat down to eat and enjoy the wine. Telling Mireille about her work every dinnertime had become ritual and gladly enjoyed by the scarred and blind woman who, no longer young either, had little else to enjoy in life, save for RJ's work and listening to classical music and audiotapes of books and lectures, especially those on wildlife and the vivid communication shared by so many species.

RJ dutifully told all. "We finally got a DNA match after I covered two interviews I had with the prime suspect, and it looks as though I might be able to wrap the case up. The DA thinks he's got enough fucking evidence for solid prosecution."

"I'm glad. Now you can get started on something a little less sordid. You said you had a problem with the lieutenant?"

"Haley? Yeah. Dumb bastard."

"The partner he assigned to you?"

"Right. And a sergeant no less. Need her like a hole in the head. Some fucking Italian kid fresh out of school called Gina something. All eager, no experience of any kind except with a patrol unit in some big city, Chicago I think, and probably stupid. I put her to work on cold cases."

"And?" Mireille poured more wine. RJ was clearly unhappy at the forced-on her partnership, but she felt a glimmer of hope that things would turn out somehow, even if ineffectual but friendly.

She said, "Any progress?"

"To making a cold case even more frigid. Sure. She's onto one that I should have closed and whipped from the file years ago. It has to do with the seven-year disappearance of some fucking worker for a construction company demolishing the old city hall annex building. He was bringing down a once safe-deposit vault and pulled out a deposit box somebody had forgotten to empty. It contained some worthless papers, and before the work foreman could note it, the worker pissed off with it."

"The whole box?"

"Yeah. The whole box. Name of Walenski or some fucking thing like that."

"He wasn't caught and questioned?"

"No. By the time he was traced to a flophouse, he'd disappeared. Box and all. Cops at the time gave up finding him."

"Just like that?" And when RJ said yes, "But wouldn't that mean he thought probably the papers were important?"

RJ had run into the same question several times when her new partner had insisted on bringing it up. And each time dismissed it as a zero. The official papers, reputedly in the box according to the only witness, a Latino fellow worker, were determined by everyone at the time to be of no importance whatsoever. Questioning the box owner, J. J. Reynolds Ltd., had also proved the stolen documents worthless.

Somehow now, however, and completely to

her surprise, the tone in Mireille's voice caught RJ short. Mireille's endless listening to her evening recitals of the day's detective work, along with listening to readings of crime novels starting with Agatha Christie, had sharpened her thoughts where any police investigation was concerned.

"It was thought that he probably did," RJ answered, but even as she spoke, and unencumbered by the presence of the brand-new rookie detective assigned to her, RJ's thoughts raced for a moment. The heady cold white wine, the lovely Dover sole, the beloved presence of her partner, all faded before the existence in RJ of the veteran detective. Was it humanly possible that there'd been something else in the box besides the official documents that had somehow inspired the uneducated demolition worker? Something somehow overlooked, or perhaps just never listed?

Her new partner had said she wanted to try to find the missing worker. Should she tell her to go ahead? Could the work and time involved possibly be worth it?

Shit, no, she decided. Unfortunately it wasn't, when you stopped to think seriously about it. The case really was a cold case. She'd worked on it herself. Others had too, including Lieutenant Haley. They'd all come up zero, so tell her partner to forget it. She was blinded by the all-too-familiar false optimism that struck so many new at the being a detective. There was a pile of more important things for her to do.

Seven

The angry sounds of two men hurling drunken and senseless insults at each other, then the crash of furniture as bunks were overturned, woke Walenski to a fight at the other end of the flophouse room where he slept. He sat up cursing. Daylight showed through the room's one window, and for a moment he thought he was late for work and had to get going fast. Then he remembered he hadn't dared to leave either the packet of stamped papers that had been in the safe deposit box along with the canvas painting alone, and he had no place other than his bed to hide them. He couldn't go back to the annex building, but he still had most of last week's pay in his pocket, and there was construction going on all over town. He'd survive a day or two until he got another job.

Yesterday slowly came back to him. Reaching under the blanket on which he'd been lying, he found the papers along with the canvas.

Almost without thinking, he laid the papers aside to again look at the painting, darkened by layers of dirt, of an old woman reading. He'd barely thought about it yesterday, but now questions about it again suddenly forced their way up through his mind, still clouded with sleep. What was a painting like this doing in a deposit box? Once more, he thought that people locked away valuables and maybe important photos, but an old painting? Was the woman a family member or someone else important to the box owner? If not, then was it there because it was worth something? He couldn't see that it could be. Who would want a painting of some old woman reading a book?

When the fighting that had awoken him died down to nothing worse than insults, Walenski rose, stuffed the canvas along with the papers into shirt and trousers, and left the flophouse.

Billy's Pawn wasn't far. It shared a narrow street in the same low-end part of town as Walenski's flophouse, with a used clothing store, a Chinese restaurant, a place with a large sign announcing that it cashed checks, and a shop selling mostly cheap household items.

When its doorbell jangled, the proprietor, after whom the pawn shop was named, had just appeared in the small front room of the shop from his living quarters in back. Alerted as to whomever rang possibly being his first customer, he went to unlock and open the door. He was a stooped-shouldered man, partially balding, and had a seedy, rather sly look about his lined aging face, with its wispy mustache, narrow shifty eyes, and a prominent chin.

Letting Walenski in, he went at once behind the counter, under the glass top of which there could be seen a score of odd objects, ranging from watches and a compass to cameras, bracelets of all sorts, and a variety of rings and eyeglasses, as well as one pair of old binoculars. Across the room from the counter, guitars, both electric and classic, shared a wall with other musical instruments, a clarinet, an oboe, and a flute, along with an occasional gilt-carved antique picture frame.

Billy eyed Walenski's rough unkempt appearance suspiciously, appraising his shoddy work clothing and his need of shaving a three-day growth of beard. Experienced for years in sizing people up instantly, he removed fingers from the under-counter alarm button. The man, he decided, wasn't a hit-and-run type but had something stolen to get rid of.

"Yes? What'cha got?"

In answer, Walenski wordlessly dropped onto the counter the packet of office documents along with the canvas with the painting on it.

Billy silently examined both. After he had riffled the papers through his thumb and forefinger, and by habit automatically hiding his instant interest in the canvas, he got right to the point.

"Where'd you steal this stuff?"

"Found them in a trash bin."

Billy was well used to lies. He didn't really care if the items the man had brought in were stolen or not. The question had been routine and had given him time to figure what to offer, if anything at all. It also wasn't a pawn. The papers and canvas weren't there to secure a loan. They were there to be bought. Purchase of stolen goods was a part of Billy's pawn business.

The papers were worthless. Just the date alone showed the time had long passed since they were valid. Only the first page or so, which he quickly scanned, revealed anything other than an inter-office memorandum about a land transaction. Presumably the rest of the papers were the same. Probably this guy who'd got hold of them thought they could be used somehow, poor sap.

For the moment, however, they could be useful in hiding his interest in the painting, which just might have some minor value. Long experience had taught Billy that the ragged edges of the canvas, which were uniform all around it, showed it had once been framed. It was clearly old. Dirt and grime hid half of it, or possibly it was unfinished. The old woman's clothes and bonnet gave it a European look. He'd had a similar sort of painting show up once a few years back and had got fifty bucks for it from Sean Foley, an art forger and copyist who had once or twice bought pawned art objects from him.

"Painting worth maybe twenty at best if cleaned up," he told Walenski. "Somebody might want it. The stack of paper is worth nothing."

"Hey man, give me a break. Them papers could be used maybe to twist some guy's arm but good. And sure, the fucking canvas's got just some old broad on it, but it's got to be worth better than twenty."

Billy pushed the two offered items back across the counter toward Walenski. "Try New Pawn. Other side of town. Colorado Street." He emphasized the dismissal by turning his back.

The now fast-surging anger in Walenski was bitter. He'd quit a good job for twenty fucking bucks? He pushed the packet of papers and the canvas back. "Hey, fuck you, man. Go cheat someone else. I want a lot fucking better."

Billy turned back, and quickly did two things. He slapped two ten-dollar bills on the counter, and then, producing a Beretta handgun tucked into his belt and hidden by his shirt, put it on the counter also, barrel pointed at Walenski. While Walenski, for a moment taken aback, stared wide-eyed at the gun, the pawnbroker, one hand resting on the gun, picked up both paper and canvas and shoved them under the counter his side.

"Get the fuck outa here," he said. "Now."

The big worker knew when he was done. He raged, "Fuck you, you ass-wipe bastard. You can suck my dick."

Seizing up one of a small pair of barbells a

client had left on the counter and which Billy had forgotten, Walenski hurled it at the guitars hanging on the wall across the room, grabbed up the money and stormed out, slamming the door hard.

Billy looked at the damage and sighed audibly. He usually came out on top with workers. This time he'd lost. Fixing the guitar the barbell had hit was going to cost money. But Billy always trusted his hunches, and though he knew very little about art, he thought the grimy little painting might be worth enough to cover the cost. He got it out from under the counter and took a second look. Yeah, Sean Foley would maybe think if he cleaned it up or finished it that he could sell it for something. He'd take it to him when he had some time.

Eight

Lieutenant Walt Haley put the receiver back on the phone on his desk and spun his desk chair around to stare sightlessly through the window at the street outside. The police chief's urgent call had come unexpectedly. "Fucking Irish bastard." Haley's mutter was half in anger, half in anxiety. "Prick," he added.

Chief O'Connor had harangued him for the better part of ten minutes about the manner in which his detectives, headed by Detective Inspector R. Jones, were conducting the investigation into the arson attack on a group of homeless shelters under the viaduct at the City's fringe. The detectives had begun to reach the conclusion that the fire, which had destroyed some two dozen makeshift shacks, had been set by the homeless themselves, trying to force the city to provide them with better accommodation. The press was having a field day.

In the call, O'Connor had repeatedly counseled Haley not to pursue the investigation too forcibly. "Hold back a little, Walt," he'd said, "especially with the fucking press, until we find out if we are on safe ground. Homelessness is a big political issue. We don't want any missteps that could bring a bunch of asshole leftie activists down on us."

"Safe ground" to O'Connor, Haley knew, meant avoiding anything that could hurt the police chief's connection with higher-ups, like Police Commissioner Amory Harris, and then those even higher at city hall. The chief played along with whomever was in power regardless of contradictory police values. Besides his own personal political ambitions and using the police as a springboard for a someday higher position of authority, O'Connor's job kept a son in college, and more importantly to him personally, maintained his and his wife's social standing.

Always on the take and playing the same game, Haley followed O'Connor's lead. Five minutes after O'Connor had ended the call, RJ and her new partner were summoned to his office.

"Close the door, RJ," he said, "Take a seat." And when both detectives obeyed, he tilted forward in his chair, forearms on his desk, and said, "Okay. Where have we got to?"

"As of ten o'clock this morning," said his senior detective, "we're waiting on the autopsy report on the one old guy who died in the fire. Cattersby's looking for DNA in his autopsy and will report on it today. Said the man was so saturated in alcohol you could uncork him and pour out a whole bottle full, and he's had slow going with his having to make sure smoke inhalation was the principal cause of death."

"And witnesses?"

"There weren't that many." RJ jerked a disparaging thumb at Gina. "She's got a list of six or seven. Mostly the homeless themselves, and all of them too damn scared to admit they were there."

"Forensic?"

"Nothing much from Forensic. They found no evidence of any disturbance of those few shacks that didn't burn. No evidence left about by youth gangs or anybody else. Nothing to indicate a hate crime. We haven't rung in the FBI."

"Okay, RJ. No need to rush it. Got the fucking press up my ass as usual and O'Connor screaming don't tell them anything. So just keep me posted and don't talk." He tilted his chair back again and swiveled slightly to directly face Gina. "And you, Sergeant. All settled?"

Gina came to life. She'd sensed a lack of moral compass in her boss the day she met him, and hearing him just now, she was sure that if not on the take, he was easily controlled by what the chief might or might not want.

She said, "Yes, sir. I've spent some time when RJ didn't need me working on cold cases she gave me."

"And?"

"I think I have a lead on one, the theft of a safe deposit box found buried in the wall of a vault when they demolished the old city hall annex."

"A safe deposit box?"

"Yes, sir."

Haley suddenly was thoughtful, his memory stirring. "Deposit box. Ah, yes. I think I remember that one." He turned to RJ. "You worked on that, didn't you?"

"The deposit-box one. Yeah, and I think you did too. It belonged to J. J. Reynolds, a financial group with key rights to an employee named Brandon Feist."

"Feist, yes. That's right. It all comes back now. Shit, RJ, but you have a memory like a fucking elephant. The investigation got shelved for lack of evidence, right?"

"Correct. Feist died five years ago. We checked relatives and business associates about his using the box and came up zero."

"Do you remember what was in the box?"

"According to the J. J. Reynolds Company, just some office papers on a long closed land transaction."

"Papers. And that was it?"

"As I remember, yes."

"And the worker?"

"Never found. Blew town apparently.

"I see. And thus no reported crime. Case closed."

"Correct."

"But put among the cold cases just the same?"

"Someone made a mistake. Probably Rothstein. The old troll's not infallible."

Lieutenant Haley allowed himself an exasperated sigh. His senior detective had turned silent and expressionless. He said to Gina. "Sergeant, there you go. You're chasing down a non-crime."

The exchange between Lieutenant Haley and RJ momentarily caught Gina off guard. How had she ever picked a case to study that her senior partner had worked on? And worse, had remembered every detail of the theft, even the names of the safe deposit box owner and the employee who had key rights.

Cornered, she struggled to justify her investigation. She said, "Sir, I respectfully disagree. I checked out the Feist guy, and I've got him back to some wartime unit chasing up Nazi seized art. And since I figured the worker who stole the box must have thought the papers in it worth stealing, I tried tracking him too, even though it was years ago, until he apparently left town."

Vivid in her memory was the day she'd found time to chase after the thief who she'd learned was named Walenski. Checking the unemployment line where workers waited at six in the morning for the chance of a pickup job, she'd got both his name and the address of the flophouse where he lived. Inquiring at the latter, while barely stomaching its smell, depraved drunkenness, and indecency, she found one man who said he'd seen Walenski with some papers and an old canvas.

"A canvas?" she remembered asking.

"Yeah," the man answered. "Kept looking at it. Think he took off with both one morning and didn't come back with neither. Must have pawned them."

Gina said to Haley, "A flophouse guy I interviewed said he probably took all the box stuff to a pawn shop. There's one nearby. A bit of canvas along with the papers."

"Wait a minute," Haley said. "Canvas? I don't remember the file saying anything like that. How about you, RJ?"

"I don't either," RJ replied. "Cops at the time said J. J. Reynolds just listed papers in the box. Nothing else."

Gina said quickly, "It's what the flophouse guy told me. He saw it. I wasn't able to check that out yet, but I think—"

She didn't finish. Haley cut her short. This time his tone was authoritative as well as exasperated. "Sergeant, nobody believes flophouse guys, so forget it. You're wasting your time. And your partner's, as well as the department's. We have enough serious cases on hand to keep us all up nights. The fucking deposit-box thing has already been written off in two previous searches, once by me and again by your partner. That pawn shop where the worker might possibly have gone to sell papers from the box is irrelevant. So is the wartime guy with the box key."

Gina knew when she was defeated and when to

shut up. She said, "Yes, sir," and was silent.

Haley had a brief second of feeling sorry for her. He said, "Good try, kid, just the same, but you hit a dead end. Happens to all of us. So stick with RJ and what she wants, okay?"

Haley didn't like RJ, and his words were heavy with sarcasm. His take was that RJ was a pain in the ass for all the top work she did. Figured herself sacrosanct or some fucking thing like that. The new kid was doing the job RJ had set her to do, dig into cold cases and eliminate some even when she came up with nothing. She turned up dry on the safe deposit box thing, but just the same she deserved praise for her trying that he knew she'd never get from RJ.

He said to RJ. "Okay, where are we at with today's menu?"

RJ's tone was flat and formal to cover the disdain she in turn felt toward Haley. "We've got a full plate. There's still the homeless fire, there was that carjacking two days ago, and the kid who's gone missing."

"Still missing?"

"Yes. We're calling it a kidnapping." A frown covered her slightly battered face. "She's only eleven and still a little young for a lot of fucking teenage bullshit, sex parties and all that, and going off on her own. Then yesterday, we were handed the idiot patrol officer who got unnecessarily abusive on a traffic violation. Taillight out, or some shit like that, and out came his taser."

Haley sighed. "Jesus. One of those again. Well, lucky it wasn't his Glock."

His phone rang. He picked it up, "Haley." And cupping the mouthpiece, said, "Okay scram off. Keep me posted." He waved both detectives out of the room.

When RJ remained, he said, "One sec, Bruce," and turned to her. "Yes? Make it quick."

"I want someone different working with me. Not this wet-behind-the-ears schoolgirl."

Haley bridled. "Fuck you, RJ. You're stuck with her. If you don't like it, tough shit. She's here on a department order. Out of my hands."

"Well, put her back in them, unless kissing up to fucking O'Connor is more important."

Haley stood up, and forgetting he was on the phone, hung up on O'Connor. "You're looking for suspension, RJ."

"Try it, lieutenant." RJ turned her back and walked out, giving the finger to the door she slammed behind her.

Fuming, Haley punched in O'Connor's line. "Sorry about that, Bruce. Unwanted interruption."

O'Connor laughed. He'd heard part of the spiel between Haley and RJ before Haley had hung up. "She got you by the shorts, Walt?"

"Don't get holier than thou with me, Bruce. Bloody woman is lethal. You don't want her up your ass any more than I want her up mine."

In the main office, Gina had sat down at her desk and was back digging through the notes she'd made on the safe deposit box cold case, hoping to find something to support her sure feeling that she was right in pursuing the case. For a moment before she looked up, she was unaware of someone leaning toward her from the desk's opposite side, both clenched fists thumped down on the desk's surface. And then heard, "Just what the fuck are you up to?"

Startled, Gina managed to say, "Checking my notes. I know Haley said not to, but I—"

She got no further.

"I see. Well, that's what you think you're doing. Actually you're not. Sister, I don't give a flying shit if you think you are maybe chasing some imagined theft. May I remind you of two things. One: like it or not, I've had you dumped on me as a partner, and unfortunately there's little I can do to unassign you. Two: we've got a goddamned homeless mess as well as a missing eleven-year-old. Both need investigating and fast, especially the child. If not, this entire CID unit and along with it our whole fucking police force is going to stink with the public. So get your rookie nose out of goddamned ancient history and trying to prove how bright you are and get to work on today's menu. Got it?"

Before RJ was halfway finished, Gina had put her notes away and sat back in surrender. It was clear to her that she'd pushed her older and more experienced partner's buttons enough. She didn't want to find herself saddled with a formal in-department reprimand. Or worse—fired.

She said, "Roger," submissively.

"Okay then. Detective-school ass in gear and come with me. First stop, home and parents of the missing and presumed kidnapped eleven-year-old."

Nine

But after seeing and reassuring the parents that every effort was being made to find their missing child, further work was soon abruptly assigned to the other precinct as well as any more investigation into the homeless shelters arson.

Less than twenty-four hours later, an official limousine driven by a uniformed chauffeur and carrying only one passenger, Richard Spinova, a city councilman of long standing and powerful political influence, drove quietly over the large stone blocks that paved the square before the city's town hall. It was early in a working day, 7:38 to be precise, and there was only the occasional person either crossing the square on foot or going up the steps to the town hall's big double doors while ignored by a flock of pigeons walking about possessively.

A headliner celebrity, Spinova was constantly gaining the attention of the media for his flamboyant living style along with his hyperbolic manner of dramatizing for his own benefit most political issues. All-too-clever lawyers largely shielded from view his endless financial difficulties, which several times nearly led to his filing for bankruptcy.

Spinova was there at what was for him an ungodly hour because he had a meeting to prepare for. He was about to consult with supporters in the assembly hall where he was to present his "A Better Police Force" bill. Calling for reorganization of an already well-organized force and for a considerable cut in the budget to that end, the bill was solely for Spinova's political benefit and was a totally unnecessary one. And worse, if passed, it was going to cripple all the different departments in the police force it was supposed to help.

The limousine slowly came to a halt. The uniformed chauffeur's gloved hand could be seen leaving the steering wheel to grasp and open the driver's door, and it was at that exact moment that the explosion occurred. It lifted the heavy limousine six feet off the ground and dropped it back down, bursting into an instant inferno of flame and smoke.

Among the handful of observers, most were too stunned to try to rescue either passenger or chauffeur. A dead silence ensued as white-hot flames consumed the limousine's steel frame and those within its deadly embrace. And almost a full half minute passed before one onlooker recovered his senses enough to dial 911 on his cell phone.

Some four to six minutes later, the square, much of its shattered-stone paving blocks covered with a thick blanket of black choking smoke, now saw the barely discernible fire engines, police cars, and ambulances filling it or around its periphery, the sizeable crowd that had gathered from seemingly nowhere.

The call came to the CID at the second precinct police station just as Gina was settling at her desk and starting to open a file on witnesses to the homeless shelters fire. Her desk phone jangled, shattering the office's early morning silence. She picked up the receiver. It was RJ. "Get the lead out. I'm downstairs. Police car."

The tone of RJ's voice warned Gina to scramble or else. She pushed back from her desk, homeless persons' statements forgotten in an instant, threw on her jacket hanging from the back of her chair, and raced for the door to the stairs.

Below, she found a police car waiting, its red and blue roof lights already flashing, and with RJ slamming it into gear and saying only "Explosion" even before Gina had closed the door on her passenger side.

Within seconds, they were out of the yard and headed for the town hall, with RJ saying nothing more, and with Gina silently listening to the wail of the car's siren while wondering what explosion and where, and trying vainly not to look ahead at the street as it poured up at her with cars she was sure they would pile into, peeling away to each side like leaves in a wind.

In less than three minutes, RJ pulled to a skidding stop just beyond the rapidly gathering crowd at the town hall square. Both detectives were out of the car even before the wail of its siren had died, Gina behind RJ as the tall detective inspector pushed her way through gathering groups of shocked people and then ducked under the standard yellow police tape already put into encircling place by several first-responding patrol officers.

Flashing her ID at a young uniformed police sergeant who had temporarily taken charge, RJ elbowed past firefighters spraying down the still burning limousine with fire retardant foam. A fireman protested. "Don't get no closer, Detective."

RJ pushed past his arresting arm, laughing with "S'matter? 'Fraid you might have to douse me too?"

She got to what Gina, right behind her, thought insanely near the still white-hot fire visible through the clouds of foam and stood a moment looking into the inferno before turning to Gina and saying, "Okay, stay with me."

Elbowing her way through the first responders, she ducked back under the yellow police tape and threaded a way out through the gathering crowd to the front steps up to the town hall front door, where she got out her notebook and issued Gina more orders.

"Note time, place, all that basic crap. We haven't seen anything yet to lead us anywhere. But we sure as hell will. This was a fucking mob-style execution. First off, look around to see if you find any small bits of jagged metal or slugs. There'd be shrapnel if the explosion was due from something fired on the limo, like a rocket. Also if you see any stray onlooker not with the crowd. Get name, address, phone. Cuff him if necessary. People who do this kind of thing often hang around enjoying the excitement."

It was the beginning of what for Gina was the most exhausting day of police work she could ever remember. Her notebook was filled with accounts of still shocked witnesses and any other information she and RJ had rapidly gathered. Two pages were filled with a precise log of the fatal day's planned activities of the councilman himself as well as meetings held by RJ to share information with both FBI special agents and officers from the ATF.

In his absence anywhere else except in the destroyed limousine, it was taken for granted that the burned-to-a-crisp corpse in the backseat was Councilman Richard Spinova, and that the charred and blackened corpse behind the steering wheel was that of the limo driver.

This was verified by Spinova's wife, Martine, the last person to see him when the limousine had come to bring him early to city hall to meet with supporters to strategize his "A Better Police Force" bill.

Gina, still groggy from lack of sleep—RJ had

not released her until after midnight—had hardly reached her desk the following day when she and RJ were again summarily summoned by Lieutenant Haley to report on their findings.

"Too soon to tell you much," RJ said, not hiding her annoyance that Haley would expect leading information when the paving blocks of the Town Hall square were still warm from the violence and heat of the explosion that had carried off two people. "Forensic thinks the bomb was attached to the underneath of the limo and set off from some distance away, and one witness said she'd noticed a white van parked in the square that she'd never seen at the Town Hall before."

"She didn't get a plate number?"

"No."

"Where's the wreckage now?"

The irrelevancy of the question annoyed RJ even more. "Just where you'd expect it to be, Walt, for Christ's sake. What's left of it was loaded out yesterday afternoon when Forensic got through, and it's in the garage, all roped off regular."

There was a long silence as Haley visibly swallowed RJ's annoyed tone. Leaning back in his chair and pretending lack of concern, he said, "Okay, you two. Get with it again today. But don't step on any political toes. This department has enough trouble without upsetting city hall any more than it has been."

RJ, followed by Gina, left Haley's office, RJ closing the door to it firmly behind them.

"Idiot," she muttered.

Gina, still wondering at Haley's weakness, was then abruptly jarred out of it by RJ snapping, "Okay, let's go."

"Where to?"

"The morgue. Where the hell else?"

Ten

The city morgue, along with the office of chief pathologist Dr. Arthur Catersby and staff of three, was tucked away unobtrusively in an annex behind the city hospital. The police car siren silenced and the car parked, Gina dutifully followed RJ up a flight of iron stairs to find herself in a large brightly lit room, one wall of which was decorated by the dozen doors of the freezer compartment. Behind them were the sliding trays of the dead, once persons now corpses no longer feeling, hearing, or seeing life and awaiting autopsy, identification, claim by family or friends, or, if unclaimed, an eventual burial in the city's potter field.

Almost the first thing that struck Gina, while being briefly introduced with a hand gesture simply as Detective Sergeant Calibresi, was the smell of the place. It was part medicinal, part Lysol cleaner, both odors merging but dominated by the pervasive smell of the dead bodies the room was host to.

For a moment, her attention to the charred corpses she had come to view was distracted by Catersby. The pathologist was a small dried-up graying little man of few words who had for so long been company to the dead that he almost seemed like one of them.

"All yours," he said to RJ. "One male, one female, probably the chauffeur. Can't say much about evidence. Traces of cocaine in the female. Got DNA on both from what's left."

Showing his disinterest—it was just another day at work for him—Catersby turned to inspect the ashen-gray already half-eviscerated naked corpse of a woman stretched prone on one of the three exam tables in the room. It was only then that Gina fully took in what RJ had called *French fries* and felt a wave of nausea sweep upward to her throat. What they had come to see, and which were lying on two exam tables, looked like elongated logs of heavily charred wood that had no resemblance of any kind to human beings.

RJ, not in the least disturbed, went over to one, and bending low over it, sniffed. "My guess, this is the fucking councilman," she said. "You can still smell bloody whiskey in what's left. Like someone held a bottle under your nose. The DNA will verify it."

And then, over her shoulder, an order shot back to Gina, "Sergeant, look into the drinking habits of both of these. Chauffeur's probably clean. People who drive don't normally drink before lunch. But check on a possible drug habit. How much she used if she did and how often. And if possible, her source."

Twenty minutes later, as she and Gina got back in the police car with a planned interview with the first of several more witnesses rounded up by the patrol unit, RJ shot a final order concerning the two deceased. "Check who did the dentistry on both and run up a file we can maybe match with what Catersby can find of teeth, if anything."

It went like that all the rest of the day, fast and exacting. Witnesses were grilled over and over, each new round of questioning bringing to light facts some had forgotten in the first round. "Name? Profession? Any connection to the deceased? Where were you standing exactly? Why were you there? Did you actually see the explosion or just hear it?" And, of course, a personal biography of each. "Married, children, any arrest record for misdemeanor or felony."

By the time the day came to an end, and after being summarily told, "We start first thing tomorrow," Gina got home to her studio apartment, poured herself a double shot of vodka, and tried to pull herself together. Her brain reeled with images of burned-to-a-horrifying-crisp corpses, the guarded expressions of nervous witnesses, the endless technical details of the Forensic and Bomb Squad report. She could barely remember where she'd got to on her cold-case safe deposit box investigation, which had seemed so alive and real to her forty-eight hours previous.

She had to get out her notebook, flip back through pages of RJ's orders on the explosion to find that she'd somehow found a few minutes to consult Charlie Fargo and had discovered that the safe deposit box owner, Brandon Feist, who had died five years ago, had been part of a U.S. Army team at the end of World War II assigned to search through looted Nazi war treasures for artwork to be returned to rightful prewar owners.

One step forward, she thought. If Haley and her partner didn't think the case worth it, so what. She was going to pursue the case anyway, whether they liked or not. And so, it was with a renewed defiant confidence that she was certain she was onto something, and with a determination to find time somehow to stay with it, that she fell asleep.

On her part, Gina's Detective Inspector tormentor unwound with a glass of wine while answering Mireille's endless questions about the day's proceedings, knowledge of which always lent excitement to Mireille's otherwise empty life.

"Was your sergeant any help at all?"

"She had to be. I never gave her a moment's peace."

A laugh. "Sounds like you might have been terribly mean."

"No meaner than required to jerk the fool kid's mind out of some down-the-rabbit-hole non-crime I told you about that occurred seven years ago."

"You make her sound obsessive."

"Guess she is. Or maybe now was. Hope so."

"But how far has she got?"

"Haven't a clue."

"It must be somewhere, since you said she gave it up so reluctantly."

"Mireille, love, know something? I don't really give a fuck. I've got a councilman and a chauffeur who are a bunch of cooled off embers and asshole Haley trying to slow down my investigation. On the take somehow or somewhere, as usual, the SOB. Don't know which. But it doesn't smell good. Like fucking rotten eggs. Always does when Haley interferes with an ongoing investigation. It's puppet playing puppet playing puppet. He and O'Connor the puppet of the chief, and the chief the puppet of some other puppet, probably not in the police, and so on. The day I find out, and I damned well will, this whole bloody city will rock."

Eleven

After Jakub Walenski walked out of Billy's Pawn shop cursing, Billy had made a small notation of his purchase in the margin of a ledger book he kept on a shelf under the glass-topped counter. Next to it he wrote the name Sean Foley.

It was a busy period for Billy's Pawn, and it was nearly six months before Billy could find time to locate the forger. It wasn't an easy task. Foley was constantly shadowed by the police chasing after stolen art and looking for him to make the kind of slip that would lead to an arrest. And then it was another several months before Billy, again unusually busy and forgetting the painting, finally remembered it, and then a year went by before he could find time to eventually catch up with Foley in a warehouse loft in a section of town that, for its rundown appearance, rivaled the area of Billy's Pawn.

Not wanting to bargain on the phone, Billy took a chance and paid a cold call, climbing up four flights of dark stairs to the top floor of the once warehouse to an unmarked door. There was no doorbell, but there were two signs scrawled with felt pen on separate squares of taped-on cardboard. One stated only SERENA GILES, the other, SIAN FOLEY.

Billy knocked hard. It seemed to take forever, but the door was finally answered, and to Billy's surprise by an overweight middle-aged woman with bleached blond hair who was wearing nothing but a pair of cut-off paint-stained chino pants. Billy was long used to lowlifes, and this one had *slut* written all over her.

"Yes?"

Billy tried not to stare at the woman's very large and pendulous naked breasts. "Looking for Sean."

"Who are you? "

"I own Billy's Pawn down on Fourth Street."

"He's not here." The woman started closing the door, but Billy stuck his foot in it and said quickly, "Tell him I maybe got something for him. Tell him it's Billy. Dealt with him before, a couple of times."

The woman started to say more but was interrupted by the rasping voice of an alcoholic. "Back off, Serena. I know him."

With a surly look, the woman opened the door

all the way to reveal the man who had appeared, standing behind her.

"What've you got, Billy?"

He was skinny, rat-faced, and balding. He wore jeans and a shirt that looked as though he'd slept in them for weeks and had a three-day stubble that emphasized his thin nose. He had small red-rimmed eyes and smelled strongly of drink.

Billy had brought the canvas with him and held it up for Sean Foley to see. The art forger glanced briefly at it and said, "Okay, come on in," and opened the door wider for Billy, and gestured at the nudes on the easels. "My wife's work." Both were large front-on nude self-portraits of the woman who had taken up a brush and palette to resume painting on the unfinished one.

Sick, Billy thought, and following Foley, found himself in a badly lit loft where, besides the ugly paintings by the artist whom he took to be Serena Giles, Foley had his own section furnished with another easel currently supporting a landscape. A stack of framed canvases leaned against the wall behind a worktable scattered with brushes and tubes of paint.

Foley led Billy to the counter by a kitchen sink that was sandwiched between a shabby-looking fridge and a three-burner range. Amidst a clutter of unwashed coffee mugs, glasses, and dishes, Billy noticed a half-empty bottle of cheap bourbon. The art forger found a mostly empty glass, poured it half-full from the bottle, and took it back to the easel and table. He gestured to a chair and nodded at the canvas Billy held. "Let's have another look. Where'd you get this thing?"

Billy told him and handed over the canvas, and Foley examined it carefully for a moment, then put it down, only to reexamine it with a magnifying glass. Before handing it back to Billy, he said, "Why did you bring it to me? Did you think it's worth something?"

"I don't know nothing about art," Billy said. "Thought if you'd want to clean it up or finish it, if that's what it needed, you could sell it for something."

Foley reexamined the painting on the canvas and said, before he handed it back to Billy, "Cleaning takes time. Restoring anything even more. I'd give you fifty for it. And that would be a gift."

Billy had hoped for more. He said, "Hey, give me a break, Sean. If you can come up with fifty means you think it's worth maybe a hundred."

Foley shrugged, finished off the bourbon he'd filled into the glass, and, voice slurred, said, "Suit yourself, Billy. Appreciate your bringing it. Which means you want me to buy it. But I don't need doing all that work for nothing on unframed shit like this in hope of finding some small-time gallery sucker to take it on consignment. Sentimental value once to someone, maybe, but not to nobody else."

Billy stared down at the canvas, then back at Foley. He took in Foley's intractable expression and knew from years of dealing and haggling with people that Foley wasn't about to offer more.

Briefly, Billy wondered where else he could try to sell the painting, and realized he had no idea. With the feeling he'd had since the worker had dumped it on him that it was somehow bad news of some kind, he drew in breath, tried to look amiable and said, "Okay, Sean. Fork over five tens."

The moment Billy had gone, leaving the begrimed canvas amidst the clutter of the kitchen table, Sean Foley opened another bottle, poured himself another half glass, and picked the canvas up to carefully reexamine the painting. He found himself looking more intensely at something he'd spotted at first glance as possibly a genuine original or, if not an original, a first-rate copy. By whom, he didn't know. Foley's knowledge of art didn't go much beyond the most famous of the French Impressionists and Andy Warhol moderns. Alcohol had dimmed his memory of any of the masters in previous times.

In his work, Sean Foley knew art dealers and art galleries by the dozen. A score of his copies of expensive paintings decorated the homes of many who were wealthy enough to buy the original but who chose out of greed and stinginess to spend far less on a copy. After thinking a bit, he picked up his phone and dialed a number for the Greenstreet Gallery, an upmarket place on Covington's chichi Park Street, a street graced by Chanel, Gucci, Louis Vuitton, Tiffany's, and other big names. The gallery had a comfortably large clientele, and it wouldn't take him long to clean up the painting, perhaps even touch it up a little.

Named after its owner, Amos Greenstreet, the gallery helped serve as a front for Greenstreet's often rather shady dealings with a lesser world, some of it criminal. None of this made any difference to Foley. Money was money, and if a client wore a shirt and tie or expensive jewelry, that was good enough for him.

When the phone was answered by Amos himself, Sean ignored the disdain in the gallery owner's voice, which he heard the moment he announced who he was. It was no different a tone from what he experienced with every art gallery or art dealer he dealt with. They all looked down on him, and he'd got so he ignored it. *Bunch of stupid pricks all full of themselves* was his usual thought. *They'd go down on my dick if there was money in it for them.*

He said, "Amos, Sean Foley. I think I might have something for you that could earn us both a few bucks."

As he spoke, the canvas painting lay mutely silent where he'd put it down amidst the cluttered alcoholic mess on the kitchen table. There was no way for it to know that it would lie there and elsewhere in the cluttered loft for more than three years before it would arrive in the hands of Amos Greenstreet.

Billy would die of pneumonia exacerbated by acute alcoholism shortly after calling the gallery owner, and it would be that long before his wife, Serena Giles, came across it lying about somewhere. This was when, needing money, she finally got around to selling some of Sean Foley's unfinished copies, his scattered-about paints and easel, as well as his few personal things, and in doing so, remembered he'd called Greenstreet.

Twelve

The press conference took place on the steps of the city hall, where Mayor Richard Sheflin, along with Amory Harris, the police commissioner, and Bruce O'Connor, the police chief, faced an implacable horde of reporters from a half-dozen newspapers, along with those overly numerous ones representing radio, TV, and a variety of podcasters and bloggers. None received much satisfaction in answer to shouted scores of questions as to who was guilty in the most heinous homicide the city had witnessed in a generation.

"Do you have any suspects yet?" "Did his murder have anything to do with the controversial police bill he was to introduce today?" "Was the bomb remotely controlled?" "Did Councilman Spinova have enemies?"

In short, and when it was all over, RJ, as detective inspector in the CID of the second precinct, where the explosion had occurred, stoically listened to all the same questions once again when they were repeated to her and her new detective sergeant partner by their anxious boss, Lieutenant Walt Haley.

After a meeting with him that lasted but ten minutes, with Haley insistently pounding his desk to emphasize the need for their prompt action, RJ finally took off for the Blue Light, a bar frequented by the police of that area, where she could get her thoughts under control.

There was a big job in front of her. They were going to have every higher-up on her back night and day, pressuring. She needed not just a drink after the rancorous morning of endless questions with no answers possible only three days after the front-page homicide, but the peace and quiet that at midday the bar offered.

RJ had never been one to play hunches. With her it was virtually always the old cliché from a long defunct television show, "Just the facts, ma'am. Just the facts." She'd built her reputation as a top detective on it, and it meant that in her investigation of the explosion she was hardly going to admit to her rookie detective sergeant the thought that consistently nagged: that there was far more involved in the explosion than the deceased councilman's Better Police Force bill.

The killing, as she'd immediately stated on

arriving at the inferno caused by the explosion, bore all the marks of a serious mob hit, the mob being a widely used term for any number of gangster organizations that usually lodged in the country's bigger cities: Chicago, New York, Philadelphia.

But what mob, and why? RJ couldn't remember any mob ever assassinating someone in such dramatic fashion over petty politics. A shot in the head, perhaps. But an explosion like the one that had scarred the city hall courtyard and tossed a heavy limousine six feet in the air? But who else? Somebody had wanted Councilman Spinova eliminated. And totally, with no possible chance of survival or leaving behind any incriminating clues as to who was responsible.

Feeding her hunch was the complexity of the death-dealing bomb and the high-tech manner in which it was exploded. Neither the FBI nor her own police department's Forensic unit and Bomb Squad could yet say whether the bomb was exploded by a timing device in or under the car, or by remote control of some sort. One of the investigating ATF agents had fueled her hunch when he'd come right out and said, "It's a mob hit, RJ. Count on it."

Without deigning to reveal her thoughts to Gina, RJ set her new partner to work on many of the more mundane aspects of the case: the autopsy reports, which revealed nothing other than that the councilman was an alcoholic and that the chauffeur was a pretty young woman with whom he might have been having a sexual relationship.

Possible semen was found in the charred ashes of her burned-up vagina and traces of it in a strand of fabric once part of the councilman's undershorts. Had they had sex before driving to work? Had her boss pushed sex whenever on her as part of her job?

That meant lengthy searching about for clues among the chauffeur's girlfriends as well as among her relatives, and boyfriends, if any, current or past. It also involved meeting bartenders to search out any revealing talks she might ever have had after a few drinks in the two or three bars she mostly habituated. "You're looking for drugs," RJ had said.

Also to Gina fell the task of interviewing Spinova's office staff. "I'll get the widow myself," RJ told her. "You have to know how to get past grief. Tricky."

It was the first time Gina had heard RJ sound even half human. Avoiding the Spinova home, she briefly but intensely questioned, at Councilman's Spinova's office, his chief of staff, his shocked and almost speechless long-time secretary, as well as two immediate office associates. Spinova's office PC, laptop, and iPad were confiscated and turned over at the police station to Charley Fargo and Ace DeSalles to search for any incriminating emails or texting.

Meanwhile, after carefully consulting a little stowed-away notebook she kept to remind her of past cases, RJ came up with the name of Leo Patricio, a minor mob member who worked as an independent van driver for a meat distribution company.

She had found his willingness to ingratiate himself with the police as an informant most useful in a protection racket case she'd once worked on.

One of RJ's quirks was her not liking telephones. "They only cause trouble," she always said. "If you need information, try first to get it face-to-face."

She left the office without informing Gina of where she was going and drove in her own car to the outskirts of the city and the meat-packing plant where Leo Patricio worked. She was in luck, and came across the short swarthy figure of Patricio just as he was heaving a side of frozen beef into the back of a company van. More luck followed when he didn't resist an offer of a drink or two, which found RJ seated across from him at a table in a rundown bar frequented by the workers at the packing plant.

Pleasantries were exchanged over the first shot, with RJ hiding her distaste of whom she was drinking with and with Patricio unable to hide his curiosity and hoping other bar patrons wouldn't recognize his lanky drinking companion as a cop. But finally unable to quell his curiosity, he burst out with a "What?" and got an answer.

"I need to know what the buzz is."

"Yeah? Heard ya. Why?"

RJ managed to keep sarcasm from her tone. "Councilman Spinova got himself blown up, or hadn't you heard?"

It took several moments for the answer to come from Patricio as he rubbed the graying three-day stubble on his face to express apparent thought.

"What's in it for me, lady?"

RJ ignored the accompanying insinuating smile in which bared lips revealed two gold front teeth. "Another shot, or maybe you'd prefer a couple of parking violations and a license suspension."

The smile erased. "Don't know what you're talking about."

"Guess I'd better make that a suspension of your van's registration too."

More beard rubbing. "You'd do better asking Mickey."

Mickey was Patricio's coworker. RJ said, "Possibly, but I'm not buying drinks for Mickey today."

It went on like that, back and forth, until Patricio finally surrendered and came up with, "Maybe Sully Yanitelli."

RJ wasn't surprised. Sully Yanitelli was a big shot in the mob world. As a front, he was a lawyer and ran what seemed a highly respectable law firm, although, to be sure, many of his clients were people up before judges and juries who also often had dubious backgrounds. "What about him?"

"Told me that there was some big boss in it."

"Bigger than Sully? So? Like who?"

"Didn't name no names."

"Just that? A big boss? C'mon, Leo."

"Not holdin' back none, chief. Honest. Just somebody big. Maybe not even mob."

"Did you hear why?"

"Nah. Just maybe Spinova played something too fast."

"Like what?"

"Like maybe he held somebody up."

Back at her desk in the police station, RJ sat thinking, long after others had left for the day. Holding someone up in mob talk usually meant one thing, and opening her notebook, she scrawled in it the word "blackmail."

Getting there was always slow work when the mob was involved. Needle haystacking, she's always called it. She'd put hooks into Sully Yanitelli next, she decided. And then what? Even as she thought it, she knew Yanitelli might only be a start. He possibly could offer nothing where the actual execution was concerned.

That had to have been done by one of those obscure groups or singles you never learned about who the mob used for their dirty work so they were personally absolved of any killing themselves. They were skilled for-hire murderers who appeared for only a brief moment to do what they were paid to do. That done, they'd then instantly disappear back into obscurity, where they remained in darkness and virtually impossible to find, like the forever unknown professionals who had got rid of Jimmy Hoffa in Chicago or the score of serial killings in Brooklyn.

Chasing after them was a waste of time. It didn't help where digging out the person behind it all was concerned, and if Leo Patricio was right, that Spinova had been erased because he'd been blackmailing someone, RJ thought, and he usually always was, in her experience, then in this case, a bigger someone loomed.

In her mind and checking her journal, she ran through names of higher social and political leaders hiding behind a cloak of respectability. Of the most obvious, there was Thomas Spade, president of a nationwide insurance company, specializing ironically in life insurance and known to the mob as the Funeral Director. And there was also George Santos, CEO of the international shipping company bearing his name and who was known to the Chicago crowd as the Terminator.

RJ decided she'd compare notes on what she knew of them with the FBI, even though she couldn't imagine why they would want Spinova dead. In their world, the councilman, for all his high living and financial gambling, was small fry, a low-level they never had any connection with.

After them could come local or regional businessmen, the banker here or there, and above all politicians, who seemed particularly vulnerable to mob recruiting or occasionally were indirectly connected.

Here, but far from realizing it, RJ was closer to an answer. As Patricio said, there was possibly somebody behind the explosion who was not mob connected, and there were not one but two people actually involved, both safely hidden in a world far removed from the sordid one of Leo Patricio and Sully Yanitelli.

Thirteen

Gina found the work on the untimely and explosive death of Councilman Spinova and his luckless chauffeur depressing. It wasn't actually the detective work itself but the endless abrupt and authoritative orders of her partner. RJ had for days been utterly ruthless in her demands and equally unsympathetic to any problems Gina had in meeting some of them. "You're not here to ask why. You're here to cooperate and get the fucking work done," had become a standard and utterly unwanted aside tossed her way by her veteran partner.

After work on the fourth day on the explosion job, Gina suddenly and out of sheer nervous fatigue had surrendered to occupying a bar stool where a yuppie crowd ordered vodka or gin martinis and margaritas, and not just the shots of cheap bourbon usually offered in the Blue Light bar haunt of many in the police department. Soft music had matched the low-key lighting and the almost subdued murmur of conversation among the bar's patrons. But somehow things at the last moment had stopped her from being seduced either by the hulky charm of the big tousle-haired athletic type whose come-on she had first encouraged, or by her own raging desire for male sexuality.

Something in the midst of it all had kicked in. *Gina,* an inner voice had suddenly reminded her. *You're on a homicide case, remember? And you've got work to do.*

It sent her home with nagging guilt and a near sleepless night of anxiety about all she knew she was in line for the next day.

When in the morning she got to the office, however, instead of some endless demands from RJ, a surprise awaited her. There was a message from her older partner awaiting on her desk. It was a brief note in RJ's scrawled handwriting that said only, "Get on by yourself today."

Gina caught Alice coming back from the coffee machine to her endless secretarial duties to ask if she knew more because Alice, more often than not, was RJ's sole confidant.

"Only that she said she'd be gone all day, Gina. She didn't say where, as usual."

It galvanized Gina. She could always concoct something to satisfy RJ that she'd been working on the explosion and nothing else. Deciding to pick up where she'd left off chasing after the safe deposit box contents, and now as much out of burning curiosity as in any hope of finding its value, she rummaged in her notes and found the address of Billy's Pawn shop, which was close to Walenski's refuge in the flophouse and which she'd noted, thinking it just might have been a place Walenski had gone to in looking to pick up a buck for what he'd stolen.

Using her own car, she drove to it, found a place to park and to her relief found it still existed under the same name, Billy's Pawn, and that it was open. Entering, she was met by a pleasant looking man with a close-cropped white beard and a deceptively ingratiating smile. When she showed her ID and inquired after Billy, he said that Billy was unfortunately over the hill with dementia, and in a home, and that his own name was Nick, a cousin who'd taken over.

Clearly anxious not to cause any additional police interest, and to Gina's pleased surprise that she'd hit the right place, he proved helpful. He produced a ledger from under the counter. In it, Billy had meticulously kept annual records of all loans or purchases. Given by Gina a probable date, Nick flipped back years of pages until he finally stopped on one and said, "Here you are," and placed a finger on a marginal note in small meticulous handwriting.

Gina bent over the ledger and read, "Paid twenty bucks to worker for stolen office papers and a painting on canvas."

She looked up sharply. Bells of excitement at once began to ring and elements of the case suddenly rushed together: Bernard Feist and his key to the stolen deposit box, lost Nazi-stolen art, the wartime unit assigned to recovering it. Could Feist have kept a painting he'd found in his art recovery work and hidden it in the deposit box with the office papers, and with the J. J. Reynolds people completely unaware of it?

"A painting?" she asked.

"Yeah. I vaguely remember Billy mentioning it. Just a small one. Thought it might be worth far more than the twenty bucks he paid mainly just to get rid of the guy, probably as much as fifty bucks. Said he'd kept it around maybe a year or more. Forgot about it, he said, until eventually he took it to Sean Foley. That name there he wrote just below."

"Foley? Who's he?" Gina demanded.

"Foley's a no-good art forger and copyist. I heard he maybe died several years ago."

That was enough for Gina. Promptly leaving Billy's Pawn, she drove straight back to the CID, where she at once again went to Charlie Fargo. "Sean Foley. Got anything on him?"

Charlie didn't. "All I've heard is that he was a small time art copier. Might still be around but I'm not sure. Ask Mimi. She had to chase him up about something once, if I remember correctly."

Gina found Mimi hunched over her desk scanning a page of scrawled notes summarizing leads in

the series of car robberies she and Pete were working on.

"Mimi, hi. Can I trouble you a moment?"

"Sure. What's up?" Mimi sat back from her
notes with a smile. She was blond, with her long
frizzy hair pulled back in a scrunchie, and had an
endless look of intensity about her, but was a warm
and friendly person without a grudge against anybody. She'd been with the department for six years.

Gina said, "I've chased my cold-case deposit
box theft as far as a pawn shop known as Billy's
Pawn and have a lead on it from there. Charlie said
you might have some info on one Sean Foley. An
art copyist or whatever."

"You've chased your cold case that far, have you.
Wow. You're the persistent one. Does RJ know?"

"No."

Mimi laughed. "Understood. So, okay, you're
after Foley then, are you? Good luck. If still around,
he's the slime to end all slimes. Yeah, Charlie's right.
He's a small-time art forger and copier. Lives with
an artist named Giles, but he's moved twice since
I connected with him. He'd witnessed a robbery."

She pulled out an old notebook from a desk
drawer and thumbed pages. "I try to update people
I think might someday be useful. Ah, here you go.
Sean Foley. Four Water Street. Good luck with it."

Gina thanked her, thought, *Okay, Sean Foley
next,* and was about to return to her own desk
when Mimi said, "Gina—you're new. Don't let RJ
get you down. Hard to believe, but she's actually

quite a nice gal. Maybe just still hit hard by losing her old partner. We think she probably has a different home life from here, whatever it is. Maybe more human. Who knows."

The detective smiled and went back to her work, and Gina, thinking, *Yeah, I'll believe it when I see it,* returned to her desk.

Fourteen

The address she'd been given for the forger was in the kind of run-down neighborhood, Gina thought, that matched where a sleazy forger would be. At the block-large half-empty warehouse that was 4 Water Street, she climbed endless stairs and knocked on endless doors before finally discovering the right one. A handwritten sign on a piece of cardboard pasted to the door said SERENA GILES, ARTIST. Gina knocked.

Taken aback by a woman with bleached-blond unkempt hair, bad teeth, and a stained half-opened bathrobe who answered, she flashed her ID and asked for Sean Foley. A response was immediate. "What for?" And it was edged with hostility.

"What for is I'd like to talk to him. He's not in any trouble."

There was a heavy silence, allowing Gina to take in the woman's surroundings, the glaring life-size nudes on easels of the woman herself, a score of other equally bad self-portraits, posted up here and there, and beyond, the general chaos of a loft that was rarely if ever cleaned or even tidied, and where unwashed dishes and glasses were used over and over again.

The woman finally made up her mind. "Wasting your time. Sean's long gone. Couple of years back," and started to close the door.

"Wait," Gina said and got herself halfway through the doorway so the woman couldn't shut it. "I think you could possibly help."

"I'm not helping no fucking dick with the mess Sean stuck me with."

Gina said, "I don't know about whatever mess he left you. Not my business. I'm chasing up a painting that was brought here from a pawn shop. Probably several years back. I know it's a long time, but do you possibly remember?"

She waited. Serena Giles stared and then said, "Sean had lotsa fucking pawn guys here."

"It was one called Billy's Pawn. I think Billy himself came up."

Another long silence in which the artist finally seemed less aggressive, and actually struggling to remember, before she said, "Billy's Pawn?" And then, "Yeah. That's right. Billy's Pawn. That guy. I remember him. Fucking weasel."

Gina said, "He brought Sean a painting."

"A painting. Yeah. I ran across it a while back."

"Do you still have it?" *It was like pulling teeth,* Gina thought.

"Nah. Took it to Greenstreet myself, like Sean planned."

"Greenstreet?"

"Yeah. Fancy art gallery on Park Street. He only shed the fifty Sean paid. Wouldn't go for what I asked, which was more than double that."

Probably paid you anything just to get rid of you, Gina thought. *Or possibly not.* She said, "Then you thought it a fairly good painting?"

"Yeah, I guess. Looked old."

"How old?"

"Dunno." Serena looked away evasively. "Maybe a few hundred years. Dutch maybe."

A few hundred years and Dutch? Gina's thoughts suddenly quickened. Then it actually might be worth something. And possibly a lot more than fifty dollars, because although Serena was a hopeless degenerate, she was good enough with a paintbrush to probably know good painting from bad, and Greenstreet had got away with murder, she thought, because she was sure a Park Street art gallery didn't buy bad art.

Gina left 4 Water Street as quickly as possible. She felt real vindication of all the endless searching she'd done and to hell with anyone who thought otherwise. In most places, the criterion for felony were from five hundred to a thousand dollars, and now more than ever, she thought, she was onto a proper one.

Her next stop would be at the Greenstreet Gallery, but first she'd need to ask Charlie Fargo or Ace for some background on its owner.

Fifteen

❧

Going over how far she'd come in the explosion case while having early-morning first coffee and with Mireille still asleep, RJ began to think she had placed the horse before the cart. She hadn't sufficiently investigated Spinova, the principal victim in the ghastly explosion in the square in front of city hall. Even though she'd run through all possibilities, then what? Who could possibly have ordered him so summarily executed? Someone maybe not mob-connected, like Patricio had said?

She made a second cup of coffee for Mireille, whom she woke to say good-bye to and to tell she was off to work, and before she had even reached her desk in the CID, she had decided to make a more detailed investigation into Councilman

Spinova's personal life, and to begin with his wife and daughters. Sure, he came from a relatively well-off family and had gone to St. Martin's, a private and elitist preparatory school. Yes, he'd married his wife, Martine, in a big social wedding the moment he graduated Yale, and yes, he'd never been under any suspicion of ever straying. He and Martine were known as a devoted couple.

The portrait of a good honest public figure, yes, all of that. But too good to be true? RJ wondered. People didn't get blown up for nothing, and although it was presumed everywhere—she'd even thought so herself, that Spinova's execution was political—could there possibly be some other reason?

She'd written the word "blackmail" in an old notebook. Someone out to get Spinova because Spinova was holding a figurative gun to their head? If that were so, how then to expose it?

It was early, the office only beginning to come alive. Charlie was at his desk, Mimi at hers along with her partner, both huddling over plans for the day's work ahead. Ace DeSalles was hunched over some forensic figures, and Alice was busy setting up the coffee machine for all. There was no sign of life in Haley's office, but there seldom was until well past nine o'clock. The lieutenant was not known for his conscientious attention to hours dictated by police protocol.

Her new partner was notably absent, and RJ, not attempting to hide instant irritation because of it, called out, "Anyone seen my so-called partner?"

"She was here a few minutes ago," Mimi offered. "Said she'd be back later." She automatically felt the need to defend.

Swallowing her annoyance and after leaving a cryptic note as to her plans for that day on Gina's desk, RJ got busy on her laptop. It was perhaps a waste of time, she thought. She could hardly imagine that either involvement in some kind of blackmail or any personal problems would bring about execution by the kind of dramatically violent explosion that had deprived the councilman of life. But who knew? In her experience, any and every avenue possible in every investigation had to be looked into, whether rewarding or not.

Searching with her laptop for some overlooked scrap of information from news clippings on official as well as unofficial biographies, she frustratingly came up with nothing new, beyond the endless research her rookie partner had assembled. While a picture had emerged of Spinova's lies and distortions that accompanied his hyperbole and his flamboyant lifestyle, she found nothing about Spinova's personal life. What were his relationships with his wife, Martine, as well as with brothers and sisters, who lived in other cities? Or with his elderly parents in a retirement home? Did he have any close personal friends?

By mid-morning and armed with a profile of Richard Spinova, along with a rough picture of his family ancestry, RJ suspended any further research.

Commandeering a police car, she drove directly to the expensive home of the deceased in an exclusive area of the city's wealthy residential suburbs.

Leaving the police car in the long flower-bordered driveway that wove through an expansive lawn so as to block exits for any car from the three-car garage, she rang the doorbell. When it was answered by a uniformed maid, she summarily showed her ID, demanded to see Mrs. Spinova, and, ignoring protests that "Madame was not up yet," muscled her way in.

The maid, cowed and flustered by the unexpected police presence, disappeared, and a surprised Martine Spinova appeared shortly in her place. She was still in her dressing gown, and her face ravaged by sleepless nights of coping with city officials over funeral arrangements.

"Yes?"

RJ flashed her ID. "Detective Inspector R. Jones, Mrs. Spinova. I am investigating the unfortunate murder of your husband, and sorry to disturb you at this hour. My condolences go without saying, but some things just can't be put on hold. I need information as soon as possible if I am to track down your husband's killers."

Taken aback and not knowing whether to comply or not comply, the flustered gray-haired woman mumbled, "Of course," and when RJ asked if they could be seated somewhere, numbly accompanied her to the living room.

RJ's first questions were routine, the answers

to which she knew, and were couched in as gentle terms as RJ could manage. "Mrs. Spinova, how long were you and your husband married?" "Were your relations good?" "Did he have any enemies?" And the always asked and awkward question, "Did you know or have any suspicion that he might at some time have strayed?"

It was, as usual, the approach to questions that were more meaningful. She received little in answer that was interesting until she asked, as tactfully as possible, the one about straying. In the first moment of silence, then in the guarded "no" she received in answer, she immediately detected marriage problems: a wife who had faced infidelity as well as probably a loveless union—RJ remembered traces of possible sex on the corpses of both Spinova and his chauffeur—and a wife who, underneath the shock of her husband's murder, was bitterly angry.

She got no farther, however. She was interrupted from asking more by the abrupt appearance of Rachel, the eldest of Spinova's two daughters, who'd been alerted by the maid. Unmarried, a CPA tax accountant, Rachel was an aggressively blunt young woman still in her thirties who was furious at her mother or anyone else in the family being disturbed by stupid police questions at such an early hour, and more importantly so soon after her father's death.

When RJ identified herself and her almost tearful mother explained that the detective had come to get some family information, Rachel Spinova wasted no time in expressing her outrage at any police presence in her house and threatened an immediate phone call to the police commissioner, Amory Harris, whom the family knew.

RJ calmly shut the woman up even before her outburst had fully ceased. "Miss Spinova, I am not here on a social call. I am a detective assigned to a homicide case. The CID of the police department needs answers to a violent explosion that took place on City property two days ago at 0738 hours. If you don't choose to cooperate informally with the department's efforts as to who assassinated your father and his chauffeur, perhaps you'd prefer to come with me to the station and be interviewed there."

Rachel sputtered, looking for words, and finally got out, "Where's your warrant?"

"Warrant? You are not being searched, Miss Spinova. Nor your home. Nor your mother. I don't need a warrant or even a subpoena, for that matter, to ask you questions. Nor am I arresting you, unless you choose to resist a police officer in the course of official duty and obstruct justice. So what's it going to be?"

RJ purposefully let her jacket fall back, and casually placed one hand on the handcuffs attached to her belt, next to her taser.

Her face contorted with truculence, Rachel Spinova surrendered. "Just ask your questions, officer, and then go."

RJ said, "Thank you, Miss Spinova," and

opened her notebook. "We urgently need to know any of your father's friends with whom he might have had whatever kind of dispute."

Both mother and daughter finally seemed willing enough to answer questions, until the questions got more pointedly personal. Then they seemed reluctant, and RJ, long experienced, knew at once that the daughter in particular was covering up when it came to asking about any stress her father seemed to be under.

"Stress? No."

"Not distracted in any way?"

"No."

"I mean not his normal self?"

"No."

Lying bitch, RJ thought. But the lie was as good as an answer and would do for the moment. The councilman had clearly been involved in something that was not the usual in his life, something, certainly, that the press had never picked up on. Questioning the short list of his good friends provided by his wife would more than likely reveal what it was.

Getting rid of the interview as graciously as possible and once back at the office, RJ studied the nearly dozen names she had written. There was the mayor, of course, and two other councilmen. There was one important figure in the murdered councilman's political party, and another who was a society and celebrity lawyer, and there was the often publicized corporate head of an important electronic manufacturing company who was also chairman of the Ninth Hole, the elitist private golf course on the city's country fringe.

One name stood out because the man's occupation seemed so markedly different from the others. It was Justin Bannerman, the third generation owner and CEO of the prestigious world-famous art auction house of the same name.

Bannerman a friend of Spinova? A man whose whole life was art. His friends and associates, whether academic or artistic, hardly seemed to have anything in common with the sort of hyperbole and flamboyant political dirty-tricks carrying-on that was the murdered councilman's life.

Looking back over her interview with Spinova's widow and daughter, RJ remembered that the daughter, in particular, had almost seemed reluctant to mention Bannerman's name. Because her father hadn't considered him important? Or because he was more important than any of the others with something going on between him and the councilman that was secret?

The nagging question was resolved within an hour when, back at the office, her phone rang, and picking up the receiver, RJ was surprised to find none other than Spinova's widow on the line. The woman's tone was haltingly apologetic.

"Detective Jones, I didn't want to say anything with my daughter present. Rachel gets so upset if I reveal any of my husband's problems with people he associates with."

There was a silence. RJ waited. And then, "He was having quite a row with his old school friend, Justin Bannerman. They went to St. Martins together. I don't know what it was all about, and maybe it's useless to you, but I thought I ought to be frank where your questions were concerned. My husband said Justin had backed off a promise he'd made about payment from some painting or other, I think one owned by Amos Greenstreet, that Bannerman had been promised for auctioning. Justin had apparently offered Richard a fair share of what an auction would bring, but Richard wanted a lot more. I think there was a great deal of money involved."

Questioning by RJ produced no further information, only a slight change of tone in the widow's voice from apologetic to having in it a touch of spite and a change in words from few to many. It left RJ with the impression, when the conversation was over, that the widow hadn't meant for a moment that the information she gave was useless. Did she have it in for Bannerman for some reason, and that much? She'd made no accusation that he was in any way responsible for her husband's horrible homicide.

Just the same, RJ made a note to also place Justin Bannerman on her list of those Spinova friends and acquaintances to be interviewed. Few, she'd long ago discovered, among the eminently successful and respected, ever had a completely stainless past. Silver-haired, courtly, considered one of the greats of all times in the world of art auctioning and art galleries, Bannerman might, for all RJ knew, have done something on his rise to that exalted status that had come back to haunt him.

Busy on her laptop, she then unexpectedly unearthed another question. Culling Spinova staff interviews held by her rookie partner, she ran into one seen as irrelevant by Gina. The seemingly untouchable Richard Spinova had, shortly before his death, been at angry loggerheads in an office phone call with an unidentifiable other person. Could that person possibly have been Bannerman? If so, any further revelations about the call might prove helpful in her investigation. Although RJ thought, as Gina had, that perhaps it was nothing, she made a note to check it out just the same.

Sixteen

Returning to the CID offices mid-afternoon after coping with Serena Giles, Gina was conveniently surprised not to have her unwished-for partner descending furiously on her. RJ, ignoring her presence, was buried between desktop and laptop, pausing only once or twice to confer with Pete Zoraan or Charlie Fargo, and so busy she seemed hardly to notice when Alice came to her with a fresh cup of coffee.

Relieved at being on her own, Gina briefly reviewed her cold case notes, then got away without a word to anyone except Alice. "Tell RJ, if she's looking for me, I'll be back in an hour. Hopefully."

Her destination was the Greenstreet Gallery and Amos Greenstreet himself. Graying, portly, always impeccably groomed and dressed and speaking with a put-on partially British accent, Greenstreet could be seen only when a client came to the gallery whom he deemed important enough for him to greet personally.

In general and to all who knew or did business with him, Greenstreet was considered "class." The gallery's front window, disdaining most of the modernists, often boasted a lesser French Impressionist, a Modigliani, or a Romantic era imitator of Rubens.

Enjoying the slight aura of unapproachability that his absence from the spacious front section of the gallery inspired, Greenstreet mainly refuged in his expensively furnished office, the French doors of which opened onto an attractive backyard garden.

Two hand-picked receptionists who represented him were stationed in the gallery itself. One was a model-thin, stylishly dressed young woman, all in black and hired mostly for her appearance and personal charm. Her name was Joanna Price, and she fitted the job perfectly. She'd been to art school, and had a small amount of expertise in art of the Renaissance, and saw the job not just as a way to pay for a small apartment with another young woman but as a step to perhaps one day owning and operating her own gallery, then to eventually getting into the art auction business, which had always fascinated her.

The other receptionist gallery employee was an effete young man who bore about him an air of art expertise he didn't actually have. His name was William Canningsworth. He came from an old family of Boston Brahmins and although in no way gay, something he was constantly thought of as being, he was delicate not just in his immaculate custom-made suits but in his carefully articulated speech and his occasional rather affected gestures. Greenstreet had hired him for his family's social standing and connections as well as for what he thought was William's artistic appearance.

Unlike Joanna, however, William wasn't at the gallery as a step toward a future but purely because, and unknown to Amos Greenstreet, he was estranged from his family, and he needed the job to survive in the city. The gallery had seemed the least amount of work for the salary it offered.

Late one afternoon and while at his desk, Greenstreet was surprised and instantly irritated by the abrupt and flustered appearance of Joanna. Unable to quickly find words to condescendingly dismiss her, he was too late to prevent her from allowing Gina to barge into his inner sanctum.

Immediately announcing herself as Detective Sergeant Calibresi and showing her ID, Gina had not come to see Amos Greenstreet without being prepared. She was under no illusions as to what sort of person the gallery owner really was and knew that the gallery was mostly a front. Thanks to Charlie Fargo and Ace DeSalles, both of whom had keyed Greenstreet into criminal databases they were familiar with, she'd learned a few things about the gallery owner of which his clientele were ignorant and which his carefully built reputation denied.

Greenstreet was two people and had been for years. In one, he was a bona fide connoisseur of art. In the other, he used the gallery he had named after himself to hide his role in a number of unsavory financial dealings that had involved bribery and fraud. He was represented by a prestigious law firm, Turner, Bradley and Sand, the name of which spelled the utmost in respectability, while the firm was actually in turn a front for the activities of one Sully Yanitelli, whose mob connections were well known.

Gina's unannounced visit, which surprised both the gallery receptionists, also caught the gallery owner completely off guard. Until she repeated her identity, he dismissively waved her off, his attitude instantly one of indignant respectability, his tone calculated to emphasize his superiority. "I happen to be busy, officer. If you are here about a parking ticket or whatever, one of my assistants can handle it."

Gina smiled pleasantly and said, "I'm here on a robbery investigation, Mr. Greenstreet: something stolen years ago from a safe deposit box opened when the vault it was in was being torn down in a building demolition. It's a cold case the police would like to see closed, and I'd appreciate your cooperation. Let's start with a visit you had some time ago from an artist named Serena Giles. If you remember, she once lived with an art forger and copier named Foley. Sean Foley." Gina had extracted her notebook and made an appearance of scanning pages. "Yes, Serena Giles. Her studio is on Water Street."

Again caught off guard, Amos Greenstreet covered quickly. What Gina said unexpectedly got him into an area he hardly wanted to be in, let alone talk about. "Giles? I don't know anyone of that name."

"Serena Giles, Mr. Greenstreet. And you do know her because you paid her fifty dollars for a painting on canvas that seems to have passed through a number of hands before reaching you."

Amos Greenstreet had by now overcome his surprise and automatic worry at being confronted by the police. He smiled blandly, making a point of remembering. And the superior tone became even more superior.

"Oh, yes. That Serena Giles. Paints perfectly awful nudes, I believe. Yes. Dreadful woman."

"I need to know, Mr. Greenstreet, what you have done with the painting, as well as what actual value you place on it."

"I really can't give you that right off the bat. Was it Detective …?" Greenstreet had decided it no longer wise to address her as officer.

"Detective Sergeant Calibresi, Mr. Greenstreet."

"Ah, yes, Sergeant. I'm afraid I don't remember. I deal with so many of these little things. But, yes, wait. Serena Giles, yes, she did bring something in, an old painting on canvas. Is that what you are seeking information on?"

"Yes, it is," Gina said. "She thought it might be old and Dutch."

"Dutch? Ah, yes. There was a fad for a while in imitating the Dutch. Especially in portraits. *Girl with a Pearl Earring,* that sort of thing. Had this Giles woman stolen it?"

"No. It was stolen long before her. She had got it legitimately and it's of no concern of yours from whom. More importantly, and from the look of the paintings in your gallery window, and hanging on the walls of the gallery, as well as from your reputation, Mr. Greenstreet, I don't have the impression that you might have regarded the painting you bought from her as worthless. You don't sell cheap art, and you only would have paid for it if you suspected it possibly had real value. So again, would you mind telling me how much you thought that value might be?"

What she said hit uncomfortably home, but Amos Greenstreet had fully recovered from the unexpected police appearance. He now saw himself in charge. There were ways to get rid of nosy cops like this one, who had taken the liberty to pull up a chair and sit directly opposite him, across his desk.

"Sergeant, I am not in the habit of discussing my business dealings other than with those intimately involved. If you have serious questions, I'd appreciate your showing me your warrant, and if you don't have one, perhaps try me when you do."

He swiveled in his chair to summon Joanna, who had fled back to the gallery front room.

"Joanna?" And when she nervously reappeared, "Would you please show Detective Calibresi the way out."

It didn't wear with Gina. She placed her taser in obvious sight on his desk and said quietly, "I'm sorry, Mr. Greenstreet, but if you don't choose to answer reasonable questions, I will have to ask you to accompany me to the CID for questioning there."

It brought Greenstreet up sharply. He knew cops, he knew the game, and he knew the law. He saw himself marched out of the gallery to a police car, with cooperation the only way to avoid such humiliation. His mind raced through what he could tell her without in any way causing himself further difficulties.

But he had to be careful, he knew. He was in no way going to reveal what he really thought about the painting, and that he was already in talks about it with the famed auctioneer Bannerman himself. Revelation could possibly tie him up for months with a possible charge of felony or of receiving stolen goods.

Innocent of his subterfuge and minutes later, Gina had extracted from Amos Greenstreet the information that he still had the painting, and although it had apparently passed through a number of hands who obviously thought it worth something, he hadn't really looked at it yet. And yes, he had paid fifty dollars for it to that dreadful woman, just to get her out of his gallery, and he would now examine it carefully to see if it indeed had any real value. But until he had proof of that, however, he was not surrendering it.

"It might be some old masterpiece that got lost and is worth a small fortune for all I know." He laughed in a way that was meant to indicate he was making a joke and didn't believe for one minute that the painting was what he'd suggested, and he added with an air of confidentiality he often found worked with cops, "Though you never can tell. I've had people bring in things they bought at the flea market or found in an attic that turned out to be worth zero, while others were worth four or five hundred dollars. I doubt, however, that this little painting that you've been chasing down is anywhere in that league, and I am something of an art appraiser."

Enjoying his renewed sense of superiority, he waxed boastful with words it wasn't in his interest to utter, but nothing gratified Greenstreet more than to claim association with those above himself in importance. Continuing, he said, "But should I have any doubts, I know Bannerman, and I will send it over to him just to double check."

"Bannerman?"

"The auctioneer, Sergeant. Everyone knows him. He has an appraisal department he can hand it to. All the art galleries around as well as private individuals use them."

"And if Bannerman tells you the painting I'm asking about has real value?"

Greenstreet gave a laugh he didn't feel. "He could, I suppose. But equally he could not. And I suspect the latter."

You're playing it both ways, Gina thought. *Why?* She said, "Can I see the painting, Mr. Greenstreet?"

"My final answer, Sergeant, is unfortunately no. Until I hear from the Bannerman, it stays with me. I bought it fair and square. So, if you are finished with your questions, I have work to do."

Gina knew when she was stymied. Greenstreet was lying with almost every word he spoke. She was sure of it. She suspected he'd already sent the painting to Bannerman. That meant the next step was to follow it there herself. Meanwhile, until she found the time away from RJ to do so, she was helpless. She had insufficient solid evidence, nor certainly any backup from Haley, necessary for a subpoena ordering Greenstreet to appear for questioning and to record his lies for the record. It would have been nice after all her endless chasing after the painting to have dumped it on Haley's desk with a "case solved." and it was bitter to give the gallery owner a triumph, even if, hopefully, a brief one, but that was that.

With a curt order to Greenstreet to "Let the police know promptly if the painting was worth something or not," Gina left the gallery.

Seventeen

Breaks in police investigations sometimes occur in the least obvious and apparently unrelated ways. Gina had hardly gone, nodding briefly and politely to the two silently awed and anxious receptionists on her way, when Greenstreet quite unknowingly provided her with one.

Ignoring planned phone calls, he let loose the rein he'd held on the hostility he'd always felt toward all cops, this detective in particular, who had simply barged in on him unannounced.

"Bloody little stupid," he muttered half aloud. "Who the hell did she think she is?" He scrawled on his calendar, "Call Police Commissioner Amory Harris about detective visit," then rose from his desk and went into the gallery, where he took out his irate feelings on Joanna. Uncertain whether to stay or go, she had mistakenly remained in his office a few moments too long while he was being "interviewed" by the detective.

Joanna had just seen Gina out and was entering Detective Calibresi's name in the guest register when Greenstreet appeared in the doorway to his office. Red-faced and forgetting himself, he shouted, "You. What the fuck did you think you were doing, bringing a goddamned cop into my office. You get paid to keep out unwanted visitors not to escort them in."

A shocked silent Joanna had barely turned to face him when there was more from Greenstreet.

"Wise the hell up, young lady. And don't ever bother me again unless the damned building is on fire. Got that?"

He disappeared back to his desk where, seated, he began to get his anger under control. *Shouldn't have shouted at the stupid cow,* he thought. *I'll let her calm down for a day, and then flatter her up a little.*

With that, he dismissed any further thought of the young woman, made a necessary phone call to a client, and then put in a call to the firm of Turner, Bradley and Sand. Waiting for Sully Yanitelli to come on the line, he found himself remembering his paying fifty bucks to Serena Giles for the painting some time ago. But with the presence of the degenerate woman somehow so contaminating the painting that he hadn't taken a minute to examine it carefully, he had stuffed it away in the back of a little-used desk drawer.

Over the course of time, however, his disgust over Serena Giles had waned slightly, and coming across the almost forgotten painting three weeks ago when searching for something else, he couldn't resist curiosity, and had taken it out to look at it. Putting on his glasses and laying it flat on his desk, he'd studied it and had begun in spite of himself and almost at once to have a surprised stirring of excitement in what he saw, and an odd feeling too that there was something familiar about it.

His interest had grown rapidly. Could this painting conceivably be a lost Anek DeReiks? An awed "no," it couldn't be. That wasn't possible. But looking even more carefully, he'd thought again, *Was it?* He'd hardly dared think so. DeReiks was a famed sixteenth-century painter of the Van Dyck era. His work had a similar Dutch look of the period. And this painting he'd bought did too. In spite of the dirt and grime that covered it, it had all the light, the subject matter, and the color of a classic DeReiks. *Yeah, it really looks like a DeReiks,* he'd thought, almost breathless. *Or possibly a copy of one. It's not among any of the paintings by DeReiks that I know, but he painted many that have been lost.*

Bannerman, though, he'd thought. *They'll tell me soon enough.* And the next day he had taken the painting over to Bannerman and its appraisal department himself. An excruciating wait followed until the unexpected surprise of getting a call from Bannerman himself.

"We need to meet, Greenstreet. My appraisal

department head was on to me this morning about the painting you left with them. It's only tentative, you understand, but I want your permission to send the painting abroad to my friend Sigfried Van Horst, the great expert on sixteenth-century Dutch painting. Where on earth did you get this thing? If it turns out to be the DeReiks my appraiser here thinks it might be, we're in for one of the most important auctions in years."

That was only a week before the explosion that had killed Councilman Spinova, and Amos Greenstreet would not have felt so smug about the visit he'd had just received from Detective Sergeant Calibresi if he had known that the detective was the kind of cop who didn't believe in leaving any stone unturned, and had decided to see if Greenstreet actually had taken he painting to Bannerman appraisal.

Eighteen

On a hunch that one or both of his gallery employees might resent Greenstreet as a boss and be a possible source of information on his current activities, Gina staked out in her car, in an adjacent parking lot, waiting for the gallery to close.

Shortly after six p.m., when the sun was beginning to rapidly dip downward, her patience was rewarded when first Greenstreet appeared, to get into his own parked Jaguar and drive away, and then a few minutes later when both Joanna Price and William Canningsworth came out.

After saying a brief good-bye to each other, Joanna proceeded to her beat-up ten-year-old Honda. She had hardly settled behind the wheel and slipped her key into the ignition when she was startled as Gina yanked the passenger door open and slid onto the seat before flashing her ID.

"It's all right, Miss Price. I'll only be a minute. I just have a question or two. When I was talking to Mr. Greenstreet I noticed you in the doorway. You appeared nervous. Was there some reason for that? Were you not supposed to be there?"

Joanna, trying to make sense of the detective's sudden presence, made an effort to answer, "Well, I—" and then broke off.

"I see," said Gina. "You were afraid you'd catch it, and did you, the moment I was gone? Or maybe you were just wondering what I was doing talking to Mr. Greenstreet about in the first place." She didn't wait for Joanna to answer. She had her card ready and handed it to the startled young woman.

"Miss Price, I'm investigating a possible crime. Mr. Greenstreet is not being accused of involvement, but we think he might have been an innocent witness. I'm not saying you'll hear or see anything different, but if you do, please give me a call." She laughed. "I don't bite."

Then, as fast as she'd got into the car, Gina was gone, and Joanna was left staring at the card she'd been given and for some time unable to move. One word kept sounding in her head with a kind of merciless pounding, over and over again. "Crime." It stayed with her even after she'd got home, and she and Sheila, the girl she shared her little apartment with, had cooked dinner, and looked for an hour or so at their favorite streamer.

And it was most definitely with her the next day when she went to the gallery. Behind the word was the anxiety: in the first place, why on earth had a police detective really come to see Mr. Greenstreet?

The detective said he wasn't in any trouble. But was he? And maybe herself and William with him? Worse, what if she were to tell the police what she actually knew about Greenstreet. It was only fragments of phone conversations she'd inadvertently overheard one day when Greenstreet forgot to close the door to his office, but if Greenstreet found out what she'd heard, would she then find herself jobless? If fired and trashed by Greenstreet, among others in the gallery and auction world she wanted for a life she'd be unable to find employment anywhere.

Joanna suddenly felt very insecure. The idea that she had a dream job disappeared. She kept the card and began to think she should tell William, because if the police did summon her, or if Greenstreet did find out she was talking to them, William might be accused of conspiring with her and could also lose his job. Or if William had also overheard anything at any time, would he be in trouble for not telling the police too?

The moment came the next morning when Greenstreet had an appointment away from the gallery. After several visitors had come and gone, and she and William were alone, she said, "William, I think there's something I ought to tell you. After the police came, that lady detective? She was waiting for me outside just when I was leaving."

William looked instantly worried. "Oh?" And then, "What for?"

Joanna said quickly, "It wasn't about me. I think it was about Mr. Greenstreet. She gave me her card and said I was to call if I ever heard or saw anything funny going on. She was here, she said, because of something that was possibly a crime."

"A crime? Jeepers, Joanna. Is Greenstreet involved in one somehow?"

"She said not. She said he might just be a witness. But it scared me." Joanna fished in her handbag, found her wallet and extracted the card Gina had given her, and handed it to William.

"Detective Sergeant Calibresi?" William read. "She didn't say more than call her? And why you and not me?"

"I think she was just fishing and thought me the best catch, since she was still just outside and heard Mr. Greenstreet scream at me."

"Yeah, that was really outrageous," William said. "He has no right to speak to anybody like that. Especially to a woman." And then, "This sounds serious, Joanna. Have you heard anything? I mean do you think Mr. Greenstreet is in some kind of trouble, or maybe up to something illegal?"

"Well, yes," Joanna said. "But I don't think I should tell you."

"Wait a minute. Why not?"

"Because—and please try to understand. It's because I don't want to compromise you in any way. What I picked up was what I overheard in a phone conversation Greenstreet had with someone. And the only reason I've told you about the detective saying I should call her is if in case you've run into something too. You wouldn't want her to think you were withholding something."

William handed the card back. "Joanna, you'd better take her up on calling her."

"Do you really think so?"

"Yes. Otherwise, if you don't, she'll probably think you're hiding something." William paused, thinking, and then added, "And maybe she already does."

Joanna knew William hadn't intended to frighten her, but he had. Thinking the detective was on to her about something, and not just Greenstreet, was scary, and she decided to call her the first chance she got.

Nineteen

"Walt," Chief O'Connor said into his telephone in a tone that indicated he'd brook no nonsense from the CID lieutenant any more than he would from anybody else. "Let's get something straight. I've had the commissioner on my neck for half an hour. That means high-up political stuff somewhere, if you don't already know it. So let me be very clear. I can't tolerate any more damned nonsense from that fucking chief detective of yours, the one with a face like a horse who's about to retire in two years. Put her on suspension to shut her up. I don't care how great she is, and I don't mean maybe or tomorrow. I mean right now."

Already sweating, Lieutenant Walter Haley held his breath in wait for the next blast, which meant whatever RJ had now done to set O'Connor on the war path. It was 9:15 in the morning, the CID offices of the second precinct were already busy, and Haley didn't have to wait long to find out what it was.

O'Connor paused for perhaps only three seconds, and out it came. "I got a call this morning from Rachel Spinova, and if you don't know who that is, she's Richard Spinova's daughter, who handles taxes for about ten of the mayor's biggest supporters. Upset her, and my job is in jeopardy, and you'll be back in uniform in a patrol car checking out homeless bag snatchers and out-of-it druggies. Am I clear?"

Haley managed a croak. "Yes." But his word merged with the sound of O'Connor's phone being forcibly slammed down on its cradle.

In the office beyond Haley's closed door, Charlie Fargo was deep in his computer. Here and there a phone jangled and the sound of laughter came from where Mimi, planning work with Pete Zoraan, snatched back from him the coffee Alice had brought her. Perkins, as slowly as he could, went from desk to desk with a general memorandum about department contributions to the Police Fund for Disabled Children. Ace DeSalles, looking more nerdy than ever in his plaid shirt and badly matched bow tie, was doing research on visible facial similarities.

And Gina, who had come in a little late, was at her desk wondering what RJ was up to. Her veteran partner, so loath to share anything with her, was sitting quietly staring into space with a strange look on her face.

Conjuring up what new torment, Gina wondered. Where had she got on the explosion? They hadn't spoken of it for two days, not since RJ had handed her a hand-scrawled list of things she wanted done immediately. Even as Gina thought that, she saw to her horror that her notebook, in which she'd kept a close record of all her cold case work, was on RJ's desk. She'd mistakenly put it there the evening before, confusing it when dead tired with other extensive notes on her most recent homicide work, which she'd already given RJ. How could she possibly ever have been so neglectfully stupid?

Gina's sudden acute anxiety was abruptly ended, along with all the beginnings of a relatively normal day throughout the office, when the door to Haley's office opened and Haley appeared. "RJ. Sergeant Calibresi. In my office, please."

It wasn't said in a pleasant tone, and Gina knew at once that there was going to be trouble. She wasn't wrong. RJ hadn't moved, and Haley said at once, in almost a shout, "RJ."

RJ deliberately took her time and followed Gina. Once both detectives had got into the office, Haley shut the door hard and didn't waste an instant in getting to the point of his summons. "I don't need you, Calibresi. Your partner is the one on the mat. But just in case you get similar stupidities in your head, you can stay and listen."

Gina ignored the insulting tone, and when RJ pointedly pulled up a chair, she did likewise. Haley regained his own and his voice, thick with anger, passed on O'Connor's order. He leveled a menacing look at RJ and said, "You, RJ. Just what the hell do you think you were doing at the Spinova residence yesterday?"

RJ knew well what was coming, but said blandly, almost with a smile, "My job. Extending my condolences to Mrs. Spinova."

A brief silence while Haley collected himself before he launched in again. "And?" He didn't wait for an answer. "That included condolences to Spinova's daughter too?" A breath. "You bloody idiot. Do you know exactly who Rachel Spinova is? She is tax and financial adviser to half the people who run this city, starting with the mayor. And it might interest you to know that she called Amory Harris the moment you left badgering her and her mother. In case you forgot, he's our police commissioner, and he passed the buck back down to Chief O'Connor yesterday and ordered that I hand him your head."

Another pause, and then in a tone indicating how pleased he was to say it, "You're on suspension, Detective. Until further notice. Violation and you will be looking for another job. Your badge and gun, please."

RJ rose and, as ordered, surrendered her Glock and her badge to Haley's desk, which being suspended required, and then said, with a slight smirk, "What about the homicide investigation? There was an explosion, remember? Or has that jackass O'Connor also forgotten?"

She hit home. Haley sputtered angrily. "Turn your notes over to Mimi and Pete. They can handle it. And with probably enough good sense not to stir up any high-end politics at city hall. You can keep your desk until I decide whether to fire you, which I will certainly do if you step one foot out of line. Now get the hell out of here. Dismissed. Both of you."

RJ shrugged, and Gina followed her out, with RJ not saying a word, except demonstrating how she felt by silently giving the usual finger to Haley's closed door behind them. When both got to their desks in an awkward silence, Gina, waiting for her partner to say something, realized from RJ's expression—now a faintly triumphant smile—that she was holding something back, something she'd missed and that Haley had too.

She summoned up her nerve and asked RJ. "Sorry, but what am I missing?"

She soon found out. RJ surprised her by replying offhandedly and with no anger, "For a start, you've just witnessed what a valid crime investigation can run into. Police corruption. Most of the time it isn't worth fighting, but in this case, I don't intend to stop."

Gina thought that was the end of it and had half turned away when she saw RJ pick up the cold case notes she had mistakenly left on her desk. Her heart sank and time seemed to stop. Now, she thought, she'd really be in for it.

"But far more importantly, there's this," RJ said. "I read all of it. Did you suppose I hadn't?" And Gina, realizing that of course she had, because RJ never missed a trick, could hardly believe it when RJ next said, "You've done a lot of good work here, kid. Anything to add?"

Completely taken aback by her partner's compliment and lack of usual cold formality, Gina let her guard down. Suddenly rethinking, and feeling an immediate and intense relief, that RJ could only have meant her explosion notes, she replied a little hesitantly, "I haven't got to the full forensic report yet, but—"

And to her even further surprise, even astonishment, she heard RJ interrupt to say, "Hell, I'm not talking about the fucking explosion. You're okay on all of that. I'm talking about the cold case you've been after. All this stuff you've come up with is great. Right up to following leads on the little painting going to Amos Greenstreet and his phony gallery. Did you get any further?"

For Gina, it came completely out of the blue. Trying helplessly first to absorb the shock of thinking RJ had read her cold case notes, then relief at her possibly not having done so, her emotions swung wildly, and she was more struck, even confused, by the extraordinary change in attitude of her partner. For a moment speechless, she eventually found words and stammered, "Greenstreet said he's wait-ing to hear from Bannerman if Bannerman thinks the painting is worth anything."

There was a moment's deathly silence while RJ just stared, with her expression suddenly and unex-pectedly changed to become one of near disbelief. "Wait a minute," RJ Finally got out. "Wait. You said from whom?"

"Bannerman," Gina repeated, still caught up in confused anxiety. "You know, the auction guy. Greenstreet's sending the painting up to him. He told me it might be worth nothing or it might be some old masterpiece that had got lost and that maybe he already had a deal with Bannerman. I didn't get any farther."

She waited for RJ to speak. And when her older partner finally did, and after what seemed forever, Gina once again couldn't believe what then hap-pened. Nothing since her first day at the CID had prepared her for it.

RJ rose—an RJ she'd never seen or heard before, an RJ she had never thought existed. The older detective who had so scorned at having her as a partner, said something Gina would never forget. She said, "Kid, grab your jacket and come with me. I'm going to buy you a drink."

Twenty

"Bannerman," RJ stated flatly. "Kid, you just shot a rocket into the explosion case."

RJ made rings on the tabletop with the bottom of her mostly finished straight full glass–size Jack Daniels and laughed. She and Gina were seated in the Blue Light, at the moment nearly empty at such an early hour, save for her and Gina. "My Spinova condolence interview: I wasn't about to tell asshole Haley that his wife called me after I got through with that arrogant bitch they call daughter. Said she hadn't wanted to say anything in front of Rachel. And here's what …"

RJ paused mid-sentence to finish off her drink and wave at the bartender for another when, busy preparing the bar for the day, he happened to look her way.

"Before he got himself blown up," she continued, "Spinova was having some kind of row with Bannerman. Spinova's wife wasn't very definite, but she got out that he was pissed off with Bannerman for reneging on some sort of a split deal. She said all she knew was that it was about some very old painting Bannerman had just got hold of from I think I heard Greenstreet and was planning to auction. She said it apparently is worth a pile.

"So, maybe I'm jumping to conclusions, but it's got to be the same painting you chased up out of the safe deposit box. All that stuff in your case report: guy called Feist rounding up Nazi looted artwork, Billy's Pawn, Foley, and then shithead Greenstreet. And now my being told of some kind of a hush-hush falling out between Bannerman and Spinova over a painting.

"Two entirely separate investigations, a cold case involving a stolen safe deposit box seven years ago and an execution by explosion last week, both coming to the same point. It's like two sides of a triangle meeting at X marks the spot. The two different cases, girl, have become one, and it can't be just a coincidence."

RJ nodded thanks to the bartender, who came with a new drink and pointed to the table, meaning another round for Gina.

"I really shouldn't," Gina said.

"Yeah, I know. Day's just begun, and neither should I. But fuck it," RJ said. "You're taking a much earned day off and I'm on suspension. We might as well both get a buzz on."

Gina glanced at her watch. It was only just ten o'clock and a workday. She'd already been through one straight shot of vodka, and there was a second, more-than-half-finished one staring at her from among the wet rings on the table. The drinks as well as her surprise at her partner's sudden change of character had blurred her thinking, and in the low light of the bar and the welcome biting sharpness of the vodka, Gina felt overcome with a roller-coaster storm of emotion.

It took a minute for her to add things up and find her voice. She said, "Yeah, except if Greenstreet owns the painting and is going to ask Bannerman to auction it, why would Bannerman be having a dispute over it with Spinova?"

"Money," RJ said. "My guess is for some reason Spinova wanting a cut of the hammer price."

"What does that mean, hammer price?"

"Auction term for the actual sum the painting sells for. It doesn't include two other lots of money that the auctioneer pockets and the public doesn't hear about. One's the agreed fee paid to the auctioneer by the person offering the painting for sale. This is usually far less than the other, which is the commission charged the buyer. Both are percentages of the hammer price and vary depending on how much the auctioneer thinks he can get away with. The buyer's commission can be as high as twenty-five percent of the expected hammer price."

"So the auctioneer collects at both ends?"

"Precisely. And that's a great deal of money if we're talking about a hundred-million-dollar sale. So, here's what I think possible. Greenstreet cuts a deal with Bannerman to give him a hefty slice, if not all, of the buyer's commission on the painting's sale, or he'll take the painting elsewhere. Spinova gets wind of it somehow, probably from some slip-up by Bannerman. We know they're old friends. He demands "in" and pressures Bannerman to renege on Greenstreet in his favor, which means Greenstreet sees himself out of the blue losing the chance in a lifetime for expected millions from the buyer's commission that would have more than offset what he'd have to pay up front as the seller."

Gina thought it over. "Sounds right," she said. "And Spinova's a guy who was never in the art world. What the hell was he using for leverage?"

RJ said, "Good question." She mulled a moment, making wet glass rings on the table before saying, "Maybe more importantly, we've got Spinova dead after he makes a mortal enemy of Greenstreet. When you saw Greenstreet, did he say anything curious to give us a lead?"

"He wasn't giving away anything," Gina said. "He's a rotten crook behind his high-price gallery, and starting with one named Sully Yanitelli, he's known to have mob connections. And probably enough to engineer the explosion."

"Probably. Yeah, that's what I think too. I know Yanitelli. Fancy-pants son-of-a-bitch lawyer hiding behind a so-called proper law firm. But suspecting is one thing and nailing a bastard is another. We have yet to find one shred of evidence to pin on either Greenstreet or Yanitelli having any part in the explosion, even if just ordering it up. You can't go to trial or arrest somebody without solid fucking proof you're sure leads to guilt.

"And that brings us once again," RJ went on, "to where the fuck are we? Suspicion all around but no prints, no confessions, no anything else. DNA wiped from the bodies leads us to where? Right back to the bodies, that's where. We've got nothing on hard drives, we have no fucking warrant to grab phones, we've got no goddamned CCTV pics. Sister, we've got fuck-all except talking to each other about a painting we've decided might be the centerpiece in the nasty killing of City Councilman Spinova and his chauffeur. So QED, as they say, whatever the hell that means."

"Latin for 'thus it has been proved,'" Gina said. "And I guess you're right."

Twenty-one

And then both detectives were as silent as the nearly empty bar around them, void of clients at this hour, and with RJ run down in thinking and Gina too, until Gina finally said, "I think I've got to pry an answer loose from Bannerman."

"Bannerman?" RJ didn't hide her surprise.

"Yeah. What was Spinova's leverage if he was actually holding Bannerman up? Something tells me if I looked at that, I might find something to help in pinning down Greenstreet's motivation. If he's really a viable suspect."

"Sounds a little far-fetched."

"So does my chasing after the painting from the safe deposit vault demolition up to this point. Right?" Gina said.

RJ laughed. "Okay. You win. You game to tackle him?"

"Bannerman? Why not?" Gina said, vodka giving her more and more confidence. "Let's review it. Spinova was known to have serious debts. He learns about the painting, maybe from Bannerman himself, and so in walks that old favorite, greed. There's money Spinova never dreamed of in sight, and to hell with friendship. He goes for it, and with the only leverage I can think of, which is blackmail. And if that's so, then what's in Bannerman's past? Bannerman may be the most cultured person anywhere, but so what? Others like him have been exposed after years of cover-up. You said Spinova's wife let out that he and Bannerman were classmates at school. Stayed friends for years. Yeah? For years? Who knows what Spinova might know about Bannerman that nobody else does."

RJ stared at Gina, expressionless for a long silent moment. A memory returned of Patricio saying, "hold somebody up," her writing down the word "blackmail." She said, "Kid, you amaze me." She waved at the barman for another shot for Gina.

Gina was silent again, trying not to let the vodka take over completely when looking at a third shot now sitting empty on the table before her and realizing she'd quickly finished it in one throw.

Finally, she said, "But we still can't forget Greenstreet. His possible connection to the mob via maybe Yanitelli. Got to look into all of that more carefully."

RJ snapped out of thinking about Bannerman almost with a visible jerk of her body. "Kid, no. That's my department. You don't want to know about the mob, believe me."

"Why the hell not?" As the bartender put down a fourth, Gina's defiant protest was just short of being slurred. "You're on suspension, remember? Mob's nothing I can't handle."

She got no further. Her partner jumped on her again—hard.

"I said no. No way, kid. Forget it. The mob ain't fucking Walenski or whatever his name was. Or fucking Billy's Pawn, or that shit-scum Sean Foley. The mob is the execution we've both been working on. Two incinerated once-people who were actually lucky it was all over so quick. Usually mob execution is just the thankful end of all the fun games they like to play with you after seizing and taking you away in the trunk of a car to someplace."

Something in the way she said it gave Gina a sudden chill. She'd hadn't really considered the danger in any part of investigating the explosion that had killed Richard Spinova and his luckless chauffeur.

For a moment until her head cleared, she was only dimly aware of RJ going right on and saying, "Think twice, okay? We've been lucky as hell so far. Both of us. And probably only because interviewing endless fucking witnesses or getting tech information from Forensic, all that shit, is hardly worth deliberately killing a police officer for.

"None of it has yet hit close to whoever we're dealing with. But when we start delving into connections and get close to the particular son of a bitch for who killing is a daily psychotic habit he gets paid for, we're getting into a whole new area of crime. Put it this way. If you kill someone, are you going to risk exposure by some fucking cop if his threat would guarantee you spend the rest of your life with what goes on in a prison? Perverts after you for a start, guards as well as fellow inmates."

The chill in Gina grew. And sobered. It was the most she had ever heard RJ say about anything, and for the first time since becoming a detective, the dangers in the job were suddenly very real. Too real.

Just the same, somewhere in her she felt another spark of defiance. She said, "I heard you, RJ." But kept the rest of what she had to say on the matter strictly to herself because it wasn't about herself, it was about RJ.

Investigating anything or doing anything that defied piss-head Haley would get RJ fired if RJ did it, and fired would mean she'd lose her retirement pension. Then where the hell would she be?

So RJ couldn't go on doing anything detective, unless she was crazy enough to risk doing so while trying to appear to be doing nothing. She'd have to be a silent partner in any further work, starting maybe with Yanitelli, whom they would hopefully get something from if strong-arming him enough or, for that matter, in dealing likewise with anyone else.

On her part, and feeling she'd silenced Gina, RJ finished her drink and said, "Okay, we've talked enough." She laughed. "Today's probably shot. So let's go. I'll make a token appearance at the office, where I'll do nothing, then go home for the day until we decide what comes first: Greenstreet, Bannerman, Yanitelli, or whoever."

She knocked back what was left of her second Jack Daniels, pushed back her chair, ready to leave, and then stopped, unsure of whether to say something or not, and finally deciding, and in an awkward way that was totally unlike her usual manner.

"Look," she said. "One more thing that has nothing to do with all of that or any other cop business. I've a personal question to ask you, okay?"

Gina thought, *Oh, God, what?* She'd finally got used to the unexpected change in RJ, from a merciless attitude toward her to one of friendly warmth and real closeness, and she felt a stab of anxiety. Was her partner going to revert? She knocked back the rest of the fourth vodka that had appeared on the table, pushed her own chair back, and with unnecessary defiance, said, "Yeah, what?"

"It's about something I saw in your resume before you came on the job," RJ said. "It's been bugging the shit out of me." She laughed and finally got it out, as though she was somehow breaking rules. "You play the violin sometimes with a symphony orchestra?" There was incredulity in her question.

It caught Gina once more completely off guard. For a moment she couldn't think of what to say or even think. RJ inquiring into a very personal corner of her life? She looked back at the older woman, who with her plain boxing-distorted face and graying hair suddenly seemed defenseless and not her usual in-charge self, and made up her mind. She might as well confess about her violin playing. She had always carefully avoided letting the music side of her life interfere in any way with being a cop, but why the hell not. "I play sometimes," she said. "Takes my mind off work when the load gets too heavy to let me sleep."

"And you were engaged to some Air Force guy?"

More? Gina managed a smile she didn't really feel. "He gave me a wave off," she said. "Or in his words, he found someone else a better wingman."

"Fly by yourself, then?"

"Small studio apartment, yes."

"Lonely-bed blues stuff, right?"

Gina laughed. "Not always."

RJ thought a moment and then said, "I live with someone. It helps."

Gina thought it sounded defensive, as though her partner was hiding something. It was hard to picture RJ as anything but alone, but she also felt she shouldn't respond, that RJ didn't want her to.

"Sounds good," she said noncommittedly, and walking back to the police station in relative silence, Gina realized that in the hour they'd spent in the Blue Light, something important had happened in her life that changed a lot of things.

Twenty-two

"Vacation's begun," RJ had said, laughing when she left the office for home and after saying that suspension was Haley bullshit she wasn't going to strictly observe.

But fear of the mob she'd raised stayed with Gina and didn't go away. In the office, she pretended to work to let the effect of the four vodkas die down without anyone noticing. Except for Charlie Fargo, who did, and laughed knowingly, but said nothing when she passed his desk muttering "Research" on her way below to the silent realm of archivist Helen Rothstein, where she knew sleeping in a dark end of an aisle between stacks of files would never be interrupted.

The end of the day was different when she'd emerged to the reality above the archives and the vodka had worn off. It was eight o'clock, dark outside, and the office shut down. She vaguely considered visiting a barstool on the way home but discarded the idea almost the moment the thought came to her. Everything RJ had said weighed too seriously, and Gina unexpectedly found herself respecting the older woman's knowledge, earned in long hard years of experience.

RJ had said they had a tough road ahead, and Gina added up all the bumps and curves in that road while getting into bed and before she turned out her bedside light. She'd assigned Bannerman to herself, and she knew she had to dig deep into his past to discover, if possible, why he might be vulnerable to blackmail, if that indeed might have caused him to make any kind of deal with Spinova.

With RJ on suspension, she was going to have to take on a likely mob role in the explosion, and basically on her own too, which probably meant tackling Yanitelli directly. RJ had said, "You'll be lucky to get anywhere with that son of a bitch. He's armor-plated."

It was a long haul, Gina thought, for both her and RJ, and for them together, although RJ, suspended, only as a passive adviser, and she was glad that she was working with a really seasoned detective whose track record of success could hardly be equaled. Even as she fell asleep, she smiled to herself at her quite different attitude toward RJ from how she had felt the day they met, her feeling protective now of RJ, and wondering how she would be able to keep RJ safely out of sight from Haley just for RJ's own sake.

The melodious sound of "On the Beach," the ringtone she'd loaded her phone with, brought her out of a dead sleep in what seemed only minutes but what was actually seven hours. It was 6:45 a.m. Gina showered, threw clothes on, made her bed as always, and raced to meet RJ at Ruby's Diner down the street from their precinct station. It was a homey old-fashioned place that all the cops frequented, just the way they did at the Blue Light, and she found RJ already there, getting a second cup of coffee from Ruby herself, a grandmotherly black woman who often greeted her longtime cop customers with a warm smile, a hug, and a free piece of pie.

"Well," RJ said to Gina. "You're number one now on this case. What's the day's plan?"

"Bannerman first," Gina said. "And right away."

"Bannerman?" RJ was surprised. "Not the Greenstreet-Yanitelli route?"

"I don't want to get caught off guard with either Greenstreet or Yanitelli, and I think I can possibly get a better handle on how to screw him into talking if I find Bannerman is hiding any secrets."

RJ thought a second and surrendered. "No appointment?"

"No appointment. Catch him unaware, and if the big man doesn't like me barging in on him, tough shit."

RJ laughed. "Okay, then, Detective, and good

luck. Can I come along? I always like to meet the high and mighty."

Gina was surprised. RJ asking her for permission? For a brief moment, annoyance surged. Was the question a sarcastic putdown, RJ once more exercising a disdainful authority over her? But then the realization she'd heard no sarcasm in the request, and that she was no longer in the old partnership, caught up with her. RJ's presence, even if only as an adviser, could actually be a real help. Gina brightened and said, "Sure thing. You can keep me from going down a wrong track."

She soon found out, within a half hour of leaving Ruby's Diner with RJ, just how useful it was to have RJ tagging along, even if it only meant confronting the big man with strength in numbers. Bannerman was known to be inaccessibly aloof, protecting himself from just such an unscheduled incursion, even one from the police, and Gina soon found this to be true.

The famed silver-haired art auctioneer, who had built the firm named after him into a giant that dominated art auctioneering, held court in the ultramodern glass office building with a sunlight-drenched atrium that ironically had once been an annex to city hall, and where his sixteenth-floor penthouse office could only be reached by overcoming a lobby receptionist of imposing authority, a smartly tailored woman who, with a nod, could summon any one or all of three uniformed security officers.

Gina, to some extent feeling a confidence she might not have felt if not kept company by RJ, wasn't fazed by the coldly formal response to her announcing that she was there to see Mr. Bannerman. Her reply to being told she would have to make an appointment was to firmly state, "Look, forget the shit, okay? I am investigating a homicide. If Mr. Bannerman can't spare a few minutes for an interview, then we'll have to ask him down to the station for one, and you with him. Refusing that would mean a subpoena for you both, with the press all wanting to know why."

The militant receptionist yielded, icily spoke a few words into her telephone, and avoiding eye contact with Gina, nodded at one of the security guards, who escorted Gina and RJ to an elevator.

"Good job, kid," RJ said on the way upward. "You might get the same crap up top, but barge on through."

Gina's spirits rose even more, and she applied the same strongarm to the sixteenth-floor receptionist, who, clearly warned of her coming, put in a quick call to Bannerman's office, and then promptly escorted both detectives into the private world of the exalted man.

Twenty-three

Not surprisingly, given his reputation as being impeccably calm even under the worst auction stress, Bannerman was politely welcoming when the two detectives were shown into his spacious executive office by a frightened secretary. When Gina announced herself and RJ as Detective Sergeant Calibresi and Detective Inspector R. Jones, Bannerman rose from behind his massive desk. "My pleasure, officers," he said urging both to take proffered chairs. "What can I do to help? You are investigating a homicide?" An order followed to his awed secretary to bring whatever drinks the officers might want.

Never taking her eyes off him in hope of registering some sort of reaction, no matter what, Gina said, "The city hall explosion, Mr. Bannerman. The one that killed Councilman Spinova and his chauffeur."

There was no visible reaction, unless an undisturbed calm in manner could be called one. Bannerman said, "Oh, dear me, yes. So you are investigating that terrible thing. I don't know how I can contribute, but I suppose something I know might help, although I can't imagine what. Councilman Spinova and I were good friends ever since our school days at St. Martin's. He was a super guy. He and Martine, his dear wife, were often guests of Angela and me. Whatever questions you might have, please go right ahead."

He directed his remark at RJ, who, stone-faced, said, "You'll have to respond to Sergeant Calibresi, Mr. Bannerman. I'm here only as an observer and unofficially. The detective sergeant is in charge of the case."

"Oh, I see," Bannerman said, making an apparently sincere show of accepting such a reduced rank questioning him. "My apology, Sergeant. Please go ahead."

Again, Gina was ready, and came straight to the point. "Thank you, Mr. Bannerman. I have a reliable informant's statement that you had a rather heated argument with Mr. Spinova only two days before he was murdered. Could you perhaps tell me what that was all about. It would help me to know."

Bannerman's continued reaction, if it could be called such, was a consistent and unperturbed smile of acquiescence. "That, oh, yes. We were arguing over his participation in the auction of a most unusual discovery in paintings by Mr. Amos Greenstreet, the gallery owner."

"Spinova had an interest in it?"

"A small share of the profits. A way of my helping him out of his often severe financial difficulties."

"You mean a percentage of the buyer's commission, Mr. Bannerman?"

This time Bannerman's exterior calm seemed slightly lessened. He hesitated and said, "Well, yes. The argument was because he wanted more, which I couldn't afford."

"Mr. Bannerman, could you tell us why he might be doing this? How much is this painting worth? From what I've been given to understand, it's on canvas and was found in an abandoned safe deposit box during a building demolition seven years ago, and then stolen and passing through several hands until it got to Mr. Greenstreet."

There was a long moment's silence until Bannerman said, "Mr. Greenstreet sent the painting you refer to me, believing it possibly one by the sixteenth-century Dutch artist Anek DeReiks. A painting by DeReiks can normally bring as much as one hundred million dollars."

Gina was unable to restrain a low whistle. She said, "How would such a figure be arrived at, Mr. Bannerman?"

Bannerman smiled. "On my part, not haphazardly, I assure you. In the past four months since

Greenstreet put me in his confidence, I consulted with Sigfried Von Horst, the world's greatest expert in early Dutch painting. We don't take chances in my business, Sergeant. One slipup, selling something as real when it turns out a fraud, can ruin us."

Gina looked up from the notes she was taking and tried to sound calm. "From what you say, Mr. Bannerman, Mr. Spinova was in a sense overcome by greed. Seeing the money involved, he was challenging your generosity and kindness. Was there some reason he felt he could, and hence the angry words?"

She hit home, and the attitude of the unperturbable auctioneer suddenly changed. He went dead silent for a moment, then he sat more upright and flicked a switch on his desk.

"I'm shutting down the audio recording of our conversation," he said. "What I will say to you is extremely private, although perhaps you are going to find it out one way or another anyway. I would, however, like to ask both you detectives that for the moment, and if you give me your word, that it will go no further than this office."

RJ suddenly spoke. "Sorry, Mr. Bannerman, but Sergeant Calibresi can't do that. She's a police officer investigating a homicide and can't conceal evidence. And as her superior I have to back her up. I would say, however, that when non-cops, we are both people who find it hard to believe that you actually had a hand in Mr. Spinova's execution, but unless you provide Sergeant Calibresi with information to the contrary, you will have to take your chances that both she and I will officially look the other way with anything you tell us."

Bannerman spoke even before a surprised Gina could. "Thank you, Detective Inspector. Yes, most regrettably there was indeed something that gave Mr. Spinova leverage with which to virtually ruin any auction I conduct, if he so chose. To ruin my whole life as well. Something he has done for years by blackmailing me for my causing a death that occurred when I was a fifteen-year-old schoolboy. "

Surprised, RJ said, "You killed someone?"

"Yes. Some said it was manslaughter, but death is death, and it was because of me and me alone that a boy died." Bannerman took a breath before he said, "Let me explain," and then continued with, "My very wealthy father kept a prize herd of Highland cattle as an amusement on his large gentleman's farming estate. It included a massive and dangerous bull, penned far from anyone in its own shed and iron-bar enclosure. I was strictly forbidden to go near it, but I often did. What I thought fun as a teenager was to sit on the shed's roof that sloped out over the pen and torment the bull below with rocks or long poking sticks.

"One spring vacation, when two school friends, Richard Spinova and a boy named Steve Randall, visited, I cajoled Steve into joining me—Richard wisely refused—and as I and Steve sat on the roof tormenting the animal, I playfully gave Steve a slight shove, just to scare him. Well, the fun went very bad. Steve lost his hold on the shingles and fell down into the pen.

"You can imagine all the rest: Steve's awful death, me uselessly lying to say Steve was tormenting the bull by himself, the police investigation, the fortune my mortified father had to pay Steve's grieving family, and the endless lawyers protecting a spoiled rich kid. The cover up where the media was concerned.

"A statute of limitations helped bury my guilt publicly, and with the media on to more important things, all was forgotten for years, except for all those years Richard never forgot and used his witnessing the tragedy to blackmail me with renewed public exposure into providing him with a share of auction profits, especially as I grew more and more successful.

"The row we had this time was over his demanding so much that it would have seriously jeopardized, if not entirely eliminated, all the legitimate profits from the buyer's commission promised to Amos Greenstreet, and leaving Amos stuck with the seller's commission payment. Amos somehow caught on and issued me his own ultimatum. Get rid of Spinova or else, and never saying what 'or else' meant. I saw a hundred-million-dollar auction going away, perhaps to elsewhere, as well as a possible suit from Greenstreet for breach of agreement, and with a complete loss of face because of it. Auctioneering is a small world, and word gets around. 'Bannerman's lost it,' 'He's over the hill,' all that sort of thing. It all found me, so to speak, caught between a rock and a hard place. But I hardly ever expected what then happened."

Gina said, "The explosion?"

"I didn't say so, but Spinova wouldn't budge. And I'm sure Greenstreet saw the millions we'd agreed he'd get completely lost."

Bannerman stopped talking. He suddenly looked years older and exhausted. Gina could see it had not been easy for him to relieve himself of his many years' unspeakable burden, and she felt she had to say something. Glancing at RJ, she knew her partner was equally affected. And RJ suddenly spoke before she could.

"Thank you, Mr. Bannerman. I know how hard it had to be for you to reveal what you just did. I don't think it needs to leave either this office or the complete confidence of the police department."

Some of the weariness left Bannerman's face. He smiled wryly. "Thank you, Inspector." Briefly thoughtful, he then said to Gina, "Detective Sergeant, I must give you some recent information that will make me seem most ungrateful after yours and the Inspector's kindness. It's something I haven't told anybody yet. My understanding from Mr. Greenstreet and you is that you have doggedly chased the little Dutch painting we've discussed as it slowly worked its way from being stolen years ago upward to me at Bannerman Auction. I have received a follow-up and definitive report on it just late yesterday evening from Siegfried Von

Horst, and I am sorry to tell you that the painting is not one by Anek DeReiks worth millions, as all thought, but one by some unknown copyist who painted in his style, and hence worth next to nothing."

Twenty-four

The Ninth Hole Golf and Country Club was the sort that offered the elitist privacy sought by those whose wealth assured them a sense of importance they felt needed to provide protection from the general public.

A score of dayworkers maintained the extensive fairways and the greens surrounded by those sand traps that challenge every golfer's skill with short-range irons. Golf carts proliferated, and a top-ranking pro was available for golf instruction and lessons. The clubhouse, reached by an avenue of trees that wound between two long fairways, featured a bar along with a bartender, loved by all, who wisely kept to himself the endless secrets divulged within his hearing distance by a clientele of bankers, politicians, and other figures of importance. A sauna with room for four was a feature of the locker room and offered, along with showers, to those who found either bar attendance or golfing eighteen holes to be exhausting, a "drying out" relief.

Amos Greentree with his self-promoted air of respectability and importance rarely played golf at the Ninth Hole, although he was frequently seen at its bar or at any of the restricted social events the club hosted. On a busy weekday, not long after he'd received a visit from Detective Sergeant Calibresi, he had made a rare trip in a golf cart out onto the fairways after leaving instructions with both of his gallery workers that he was on a personal call to a nameless client.

When he had reached a five iron distance from the sixth green, he parked in the shade of some copper beech trees that fringed the long carefully groomed fairway and waited. In a few minutes another golf cart appeared. Driving it was Justin Bannerman, who had left instructions with his secretary that he was off on personal business and would take no calls until he was back, which would be before lunch.

Neither Bannerman nor Greenstreet were dressed for golfing. Both had left their cell phones securely safe in their respective clubhouse lockers. What they met about and what they had to say to each other was something they wanted nobody to hear, and they parked close, golf carts facing opposite directions, so that both drivers were only a foot or so apart and there was no need for raised voices in order to be heard.

"Your call from Siegfried," Greenstreet said after cautiously looking about to see that no golfer was nearby. "You think his word is absolute?"

"Amos, Siegfried Von Horst is hands-down the number-one world expert on DeReiks. And he said this—he said he might somehow be able to call it a DeReiks by nature of the brushstrokes, but that clearly to an educated eye, it was an imitation, by some unknown artist—and he stressed unknown—that no astute prospective buyer would ever be willing to fork out serious money for."

"In short," Amos said, "I do not have a lost masterpiece worth millions up for auction." The realization had fallen like an ax, and Greenstreet let it linger a moment before he said, "of course, that doesn't have to be."

"Your point?"

"My point is," Amos said carefully, "that I can get the painting cleaned and completed by a copyist. The seated woman reading a book lacks half the book, for example, and her bonnet appears unfinished. I could then sell the painting as a bona fide antique by an unknown for a few thousand. Or ..."

Greenstreet paused. There was another silence before the art dealer spoke again, a silence broken only by the swish of a golf club and the click of its iron as a golfer, not far away, shot for the fifth green.

"Or," Greenstreet continued, "Instead of an

auction for a hundred million, and if you for some reason of conscience feel duty bound to have a sale at all, you can simply sell it to yourself anonymously at a token price through the convenience of a couple of your tax-exempt Caribbean shell companies."

There was another long silence. Then Bannerman said, "That would be fraud." It was said more as a matter of fact than in a tone of shock.

"Possibly, if somehow ever discovered," Greenstreet said, "but an entirely avoidable risk, which gets us to the point."

After a moment's silence, Bannerman spoke again, but with difficulty. Looking at the smiling Greenstreet, he had begun to see Greenstreet's ploy. "Which is?" he asked.

"We both expected a big auction profit," Greenstreet replied. "I would still expect my full share."

And so that was it, Bannerman realized, now fully aware of how he would be had by such a scheme, rewarding only Greenstreet. "At a loss to me," he declared flatly, "of around some twenty five million via a money transfer to you of the buyer's entire sales commission from a supposed hundred-million-dollar auction."

"It only seems fair," Greenstreet said, adding a smug and superior smile he didn't bother to suppress. "It was what was agreed on when we both thought the painting worth millions and, of course, until your friend Spinova came along, through no fault of mine." A pause, before he added pointedly,

"Need I say that leaves me as the only one who knows your blackmail problem with him? Which, incidentally, I had eliminated for you at not inconsiderable expense to myself."

When the two golf carts drove away from under the copper beech trees, Amos Greentree was potentially close to twenty five million dollars richer. And Bannerman dully realized he'd got rid of one blackmailer perhaps only to find himself saddled with another.

Twenty-five

Bannerman's casual revelation that the painting on canvas she had so long pursued as a possible felony was close to worthless had fallen heavily on Gina. Totally unprepared for it, she managed, however, to maintain her cool and proper professional appearance and didn't let her severe disappointment show until she and RJ were safely away from the interview. At the wheel of the police car in which they were returning to their CID offices, she let loose, pounding the steering wheel over and over in an unleashed outpouring of fury while screaming, "Damn, damn, damn."

A silent RJ patiently let her run down before she said quietly, "Yeah, I agree. But it's win some, lose some, kid. Happens to all of us. And you have hardly wasted your time. You don't have the felony you thought you were chasing, but we are nine fucking steps farther in nailing down whoever was responsible for murdering Councilman Spinova than we were. That's only because of you and your never-give-up work on the cold case that everyone, especially me, laughed at. Go figure that someone who painted a fucking picture hundreds of years ago could point a finger today at some bastard who planted a bomb."

After that, RJ was silent until parking outside the police station, and when starting to get out of the police car, she said, "Okay, back at it. You've got work to do, kid, so let's not shed any more tears over past disappointments, and dig into now."

It was only because of RJ that Gina was able to pull herself together. In a very short period she had learned what a partnership in detective work could mean. She and RJ were thinking alike on the case. She'd hardly reached her desk when she also realized how "back with it" she was. A scrawled note from Mimi Parker said that someone called Joanna Price, "to whom you gave your card," had called. And Mimi had written a telephone number.

Gina called the number at once. It was Joanna's cell phone, and when Joanna answered, she said. "Joanna, this is Detective Sergeant Calibresi. How soon can you come and see me?"

Sunday morning thus found Joanna in the interview room at the CID of Covington's second police precinct. Of standard design everywhere, the soundproof room downstairs was monitored by cameras and by audio mikes mounted inconspicuously on its otherwise bare walls. Access to it was by one door only, which in turn led to a corridor near the adjacent basement archives. Its isolation was deliberately conceived to keep any person being interviewed from the reality of the world outside it, making them feel vulnerable and more likely to disclose whatever information sought.

Joanna, seated at the table, felt that time had frozen. Heart in mouth, she had finally summoned the courage to call Detective Sergeant Calibresi. There'd been the last anxious hesitation outside the police station door, the embarrassed question when she finally went in as to where she could find the detective with whom she had an appointment, then finding herself ushered by a surprisingly friendly young man named Fargo past a number of desks, some busy, some Sunday empty. Reaching the one he'd escorted her to, she was met by the detective herself, who said how glad she was she had come. And then before she knew it, she'd been taken down to this soulless little room where she was left alone for a few minutes when the detective said she'd bring a couple of coffees and be right back.

Plunking the two mugs down on the table the moment she returned, Gina wasted no time in getting into the interview. After telling Joanna once more how very much she appreciated her decision to come and that she had absolutely nothing to fear in helping the police in a serious investigation, she got right into it.

"Miss Price, my impression of Mr. Greenstreet is that he can't be an easy man to work for. Am I right?"

The detective's pleasant welcoming demeanor had begun to relax Joanna, although her twisting one hand in the other still revealed her nervousness at being where she was, and the lingering feeling that she shouldn't be there, that she was somehow wrong for ever calling the detective regardless of William urging she should.

She managed an answer. "Well, yes, he is, I guess."

"In what way, Joanna? Has he harassed you?"

"Oh, no. I wouldn't have stayed in the gallery one minute if he ever did."

"I meant verbally abused. Has he been unfair or accusatory over things you might have done that he disapproved of?" Gina paused to sip coffee before she continued. "Did my request you call me give you a chance to get even with him about something?"

The question jarred Joanna out of any lingering discomfort. She felt a surge of anger and answered in a raised voice. "No. Not at all. I'm not the kind of person to call the police about anything like that. But his shouting obscenities at me made me so angry I began to sort of take revenge, I guess, by spying on him."

"Spying? How?"

"Well, mostly listening to his phone conversations whenever he leaves his office door open. And then also checking what calls he makes on his cell phone when he goes out and forgets and leaves the phone on his desk."

With what she knew from her own personal contact with Amos Greenstreet, Gina had already formed a picture of the art gallery owner as being so self-centered and disdainful of anyone beneath him as to assume his private affairs were off-limits from others and to take little precaution against snooping.

She offered Joanna a conspiratorial light laugh and said, "That's understandable. I'm sure I would have done the same." And waited.

"Well," Joanna began, "I overheard a phone conversation, at least some of it, Mr. Greenstreet had with someone in which he was so angry that he forgot to close his office door. I couldn't not hear it. And it was so weird I thought it probably had to be the reason you had come to see him."

"Go ahead. Can you tell me what you heard?"

"He was talking to someone called Sully. And I can't remember his exact words, but I think he was furious with this Sully because he said Sully still hadn't paid out the money for the job he'd ordered him to do. He said he'd paid this Sully person a lot and he'd better make certain he didn't get any kickback from the guys in Chicago Sully had got to do a job."

"In Chicago?"

"Yes."

"That's all? Are you sure you didn't get this

Sully's full name?"

"Not then, no. But later when I had a quick look at his cell phone he'd left on his desk, I saw he'd made two calls at the same time I'd overheard him talking to this Sully person. They were to someone called Turner something. I can't remember the full name but there were three of them, so I guess some kind of a company."

"Turner, Bradley and Sand?"

Joanna's expression showed her surprise, "Well, yes, something like that."

And Gina thought, *Jackpot. And I'm getting this because of chasing up a painting found in a safe deposit box? I can't believe it.* And almost simultaneously knew RJ would be looking down at her, and Joanna and hearing every word, and trying to absorb the completely unexpected herself. The cold case she'd so sneered at was possibly leading to providing evidence in the Spinova homicide? Impossible. But there it was.

Gina reached across the table to put a hand on one of Joanna's. "Joanna, what you heard is very important, and I am ever so appreciative of you coming and telling me about it. Was there anything else said?"

"I can't remember anything else, because I think Mr. Greenstreet realized that either I or William could hear what he was saying. He looked my way, and kicked the door shut hard."

"Oh? And so that was that?"

"I guess. Only William might have heard something I didn't."

"William is the young man I saw in the gallery?"

"Yes."

"Would he be willing to come see me, do you think?"

"I can ask him, but William is scared stiff of your thinking he might be part of why you came to see Mr. Greenstreet in the first place."

Gina glanced upward at the one-way window, again knowing RJ had overheard every word and knowing that RJ would do, just as she planned to do herself.

She returned her attention to Joanna. "Joanna, thank you again. And what I have to say is just to warn you, and your friend William, not to be alarmed if you see me at the gallery again. It will have nothing at all to do with you, but it will probably be with a search warrant."

Twenty-six

Gina found a rarely smiling RJ waiting for her when she emerged to have Joanna escorted either back to work or to her home, whichever she preferred.

"Good job," was what the older woman first said, and then mentally adding things up, went on with, "So Greenstreet has financed Sully Yanitelli into paying somebody in Chicago. That could only mean the Chicago Six mob. When we have search and seize warrants, we'll check that out. The Six hides behind a company called Spartan Ltd. Yeah, all very neat, but it's still fucking hearsay, dammit, no matter how you slice it. You're going to need to lay hands on some hard evidence. Let's get Fargo's and DeSalles's take on it."

The two tech experts had been watching the

whole Joanna interview on a special computer monitor on Ace's desk that could be used as a backup to what was seen through the one-way window above the room, recording both sound and visually every moment of what went on.

Enjoying fresh coffee brought to her desk by Alice and after getting both men's take on what they had watched, Gina reflected a moment and said, "I'm seeing Haley, because like it or not, I can't move an inch more without bringing him in. I can't go over his head for warrants and all the necessary backup force for search and seizure of phones and computers as well as arresting Greenstreet and Yanitelli. I'm going to need help from you guys. And it's right now, not tomorrow."

"Count me in," Charlie said.

Ace didn't need to be asked twice. If nothing else, he loved putting down Haley with cold facts the lieutenant could neither dispute nor override. He said, "Sure fire, kid," and after quickly downloading Joanna's interview onto a thumb drive, followed Gina, RJ, and Charlie Fargo into Haley's office.

Caught off guard by a battalion of his staff barging in unannounced, the lieutenant was immediately flustered and sputtered out, "What the hell is this? I didn't ask for all of you."

Gina wasted no time. She said, "We have a suspect in the Spinova homicide, Lieutenant."

Haley overcame his stammered surprise and managed to ask, "You what?"

Charlie Fargo answered. "The detectives have rooted out the guilty in the explosion case, Lieutenant."

"It's all on here," Ace said, holding up the thumb drive and then putting it into Haley's computer. "Take a look. Whistleblower, name of Joanna Price, employee in the Amos Greenstreet Gallery on Park Street, who was interviewed today."

Alarm appeared in Haley's expression. "Greenstreet? Hey, slow down," he said. "Amos Greenstreet? Are you kidding? I'm going to have to clear any action there with O'Connor or higher, the commissioner. Greenstreet has friends who are power brokers in this city." He turned from Ace and Charlie Fargo to scowl at Gina. "Greenstreet tied to the explosion? Is this another of your fancy rookie ideas? Well, lay off it. And right now. One word you're after Greenstreet and we'll have the press all over us. How the hell did you connect him to the Spinova homicide, anyway? Have you gone crazy?"

"I got to him," Gina replied, "when chasing up the safe deposit box cold case you told me to quit. Specifically in following to Greenstreet a small painting on canvas that had been in the box when the worker ran off with it, and looked to be by the sixteenth-century Dutch artist Anek DeReiks, and possibly worth a fortune. But take a look at the interview Ace recorded."

Before Haley could come back at her, Ace clicked on the audio of the interview, and unable to resist, Haley began to watch the video on his monitor as Joanna's hesitant words filled his office.

When it was over, Haley managed to respond, but grudgingly, "Okay. Sounds good, I guess. But it's not evidence. It's total hearsay."

"Not when you know what's happened to the little painting I chased down, Lieutenant," Gina said. "Greenstreet's been dealing with Bannerman, who thought he could sell it for millions. And we have evidence from Bannerman himself, whom we just interviewed, that Spinova was blackmailing him for a cut that would have robbed Greenstreet of most if not all of his share of the profit. All of which matched up with what you just heard the young gallery lady say."

Haley slowly took it in, and then for the first time seemed aware of RJ, who had chosen an unobtrusive seat near his door to sit silently. "Wait a minute," he said, his voice rising. "We? Just who the hell is we?"

"My partner," Gina said. "Detective Inspector RJ. And I'd appreciate your taking her off suspension immediately."

Haley flared. "Are you kidding, young lady? No way."

RJ suddenly spoke, and for the first time. Her tone was quiet but firm. "Hey, Lieutenant, slow down, okay? Let's sort something out. You don't like me any more than I don't like you. We're a mutual hate club. But we have an especially nasty homicide on our hands, with the commissioner, the mayor, and the press all screaming, and Sergeant

Calibresi has come up with real evidence, the first time anybody has. We need to go after it right now. So a truce, okay? And that means reinstating me because I'm sure you can't want her walking by herself into an almost definite mob operation, given who Yanitelli is."

Haley's expression of hostility toward RJ began to lessen before a grudging knowledge of her endless career successes lent assurance that the gallery employee's information linked to Bannerman's statement was more likely than not bona fide evidence. It would be the first in the case that had O'Connor all over him, demanding action, and he saw a chance to get the police chief off his back for once.

Charlie Fargo spoke up. "Lieutenant, my experience with Sergeant Calibresi is that when she says she has evidence of something, she does. And I don't think this case can risk another day in doubting her. If we do nothing and the press gets hold of this, which they assuredly will, we'll come across like fucking idiots, and maybe all be out looking for jobs."

It gave Haley the excuse to save face. He surrendered reluctantly. "All right, then. Get on with it. Sergeant, it's pretty much your baby, and I guess RJ's too. What's next?"

Gina spoke up. "We need to coordinate with the Chicago police. That's where the mob is that Yanitelli is paying off for Spinova's execution. Best bet is the Chicago Six. They have a history of involvement in past explosions. And we're going to collect

CCTV on their cars for the past three months, here around City Hall as well as in Chicago outside their firm, which is called Spartan Ltd."

RJ said, "And we'll need CCTV footage on Greenstreet as well, Lieutenant. We'll need search warrants for both Greenstreet and Yanitelli. We'll need their laptops and cell phones to see what we're pretty sure will verify Chicago's role, and I'd like anything obscure covered, like fingerprints on the wooden benches at the edge of the Town Hall square. We don't know but what one of the bombers might have sat on one at some time while doing their planning."

Haley said, "I'll have a word with the DA, see what judge he thinks best for the warrants. What's the firm Yanitelli is a lawyer at?"

"Turner, Bradley and Sand."

Haley let out a low whistle. "Jesus. Yeah, the biggest. Is that where you plan to nail him?"

RJ laughed, knowing Haley had just visualized the office tower hosting the Ivy League firm behind which Yanitelli, the firm's real power, conveniently hid. "We'll get him at home to keep upsetting people to a minimum."

Haley looked relieved, and Gina knew that in spite of going along with search and seizure, the shadow of O'Connor still lurked over the lieutenant.

Haley's office was quickly filled when Haley called a general meeting of all the CID staff and wasted no time in telling everyone they were trying for a big hit and warned that everyone shouldn't take even a hint of this home. "Wives and children or partners not excused," he said. "Keep your houses or apartments locked when not there. We can't take any chances on a leak to the press destroying any surprise raid, or either Yanitelli or Greenstreet being somehow forewarned."

The meeting lasted several hours. The FBI in the person of special agent Bill Dennison was rung in and briefed. Everyone then went to work planning. It was only a week since Councilman Spinova had met his fate.

When Gina finally got home to her tiny studio apartment, it was late. She was exhausted from all the tension that had begun so early in the day and lasted so long. But she felt good, and for the first time, she felt she really belonged, and was no longer a rookie on a wild goose chase after a painting in a stolen safe deposit box.

She had a drink, relaxed, and passed on going to a bar for a random hookup. Instead she got out her violin and played for a while, first part of a Beethoven concerto she loved, and then some of Vivaldi's *Four Seasons*.

The music drifted through walls throughout her floor, and one resident, hearing it, said to herself, *Go figure. And all this time I thought the lady was a cop.*

Twenty-seven

❦

Two days later, search and seizure raids took place at the wealthy suburban homes of both Amos Greenstreet and Sully Yanitelli. At three a.m. in the dark and moonless predawn, police descended on both the homes, maintaining dead silence until they kicked open doors and swarmed inside, shouting, "Police," and rousting out unsuspecting sleepers in pajamas to hustle them into a waiting police van, which would take those marked for immediate arrest to police holding cells.

In spite of every precaution, word had somehow leaked to the press, and in a surreal drama, photographers gleefully took pictures of both Greenstreet and Yanitelli, noting their tousled hair and unshaved appearances, so different from their usual public images. Greenstreet, the idol of rich art seekers, and Yanitelli, the austere gray-haired senior statesman lawyer, always impeccably groomed, were both followed by equally disheveled wives and daughters, several wearing nightgowns and T-shirts.

At the CID offices, Lieutenant Haley, his detectives, and forensic and data specialists pored over seized laptops, cell phones, and iPads, coming up within twelve hours with a trove of information allowing the Chicago police to strike the Chicago Six in its Spartan Ltd. headquarters. The Chicago newspapers followed with photographs of a half-dozen long-known gangsters, handcuffed hands behind their backs and heads bowed or covered, being packed into a waiting van.

And on the day following the raid, Covington's mayor appeared on the steps of Covington's city hall to address a large assembly of the press. With him were Police Commissioner Amory Harris, who wore his medal-spattered and police insignia uniform, and Police Chief Bruce O'Connor.

"Your city police," Mayor Richard Sheflin declared, addressing a wall of mikes and slanting all his remarks to cast credit on himself, "are proud to have tracked down the perpetrators of this heinous crime that occurred only one week ago where you are now standing, and which took the lives of Councilman Spinova and his chauffeur."

"Asshole," RJ muttered, watching the mayor on TV along with Gina and much of the office staff, whose intelligence and tech skill combined with tireless efforts had helped to bring justice down on the crime.

"We got both the guilty here," Gina had said in summarizing the raids in Haley's office when a report to both the DA and the police commissioner was being prepared. "My guess is we now have enough hard evidence for the DA to ask the court to put Greentree away for ten years for aiding and abetting, and Yanitelli for a minimum of twenty for his part in ordering the homicide."

"How about Chicago?" Haley asked.

"Up to the DA there," Gina said. "I talked to Bill Dennison this morning when he called with the FBI report, and he says the Chicago police, along with himself and some guys from ATF got in at least half of the Six gang."

Haley had immediately worn a worried look. "Only half? Best watch yourselves, then, both of you. The mob knows who is responsible and they'll be looking for vengeance."

Later, after celebratory drinks with Charlie Fargo, Mimi, Pete, and Ace DeSalles, and preparing to leave the Blue Light and call it a day, RJ stopped Gina. "You're not going home."

"Oh? What's up?"

RJ said, "What's up is that you're spending the next week, perhaps longer, in the protection of a hotel. I've booked you a room. You can go home now only to collect some things and then that's it, okay? And in case you feel like arguing, it's Haley's idea as well as mine. And also O'Connor's. In short, it's an order."

It was useless to protest, Gina knew. "What about yourself?" she asked.

"I'm shipping off to a friend in the country who Chicago doesn't know about," RJ responded flatly.

"Where's that?"

RJ turned away and didn't reply, and Gina, sensing that for some reason she shouldn't ask further, didn't pursue it.

Within an hour, Gina dutifully collected some personal things, locked her tiny studio apartment, and checked into the hotel RJ had picked. It was the best one in town, and the lobby so sumptuous and the staff so trained and courteous that Gina felt she really didn't belong there. Years of being working-class had left her unprepared for the expensively dressed upmarket clientele who seemed to accept being there as an inalienable right.

Surrendering, Gina forced herself to enjoy the luxury of the room assigned, the safety of her locked door, and the presence of the police officer posted to assure that safety. But she didn't sleep well in it. Something nagged, and the third night there, she was still awake at two a.m. She missed her tiny apartment, her pictures on the dresser, her violin, yes. But it wasn't really any of that. And she finally faced what it was that kept her awake.

It was RJ saying she'd be staying with a friend in the country. There'd been something unnatural in the way she'd said it, and at the time more concerned with putting up at a hotel herself, Gina realized that she'd unthinkingly shrugged it off as just the abrupt way RJ spoke.

Gina had started to know RJ well, and she didn't remember RJ ever mention knowing someone who lived in the country outside Covington. She was quite sure of it. Country and RJ just didn't fit.

Now she was overtaken by doubt, mentally replaying the moment over and over until sleep was impossible. RJ had indeed lied, she was sure of it. RJ had packed her away to safety but had no intention of doing the same for herself. For some reason, she didn't want to. But why? She'd once said, Gina remembered, that she lived with someone. Was that it? Could it be some old or invalided person who couldn't be safely moved?

Whatever the reason, RJ had back her Glock that she'd surrendered to Haley; she also had her wits and years of police experience in which she'd faced just about every danger imaginable. Convinced she'd be okay, she had let her guard down, Gina could not stop thinking, and had decided that she was more than able to protect herself and the person she'd said she lived with.

A stronger bond than Gina ever could have imagined had formed between her and the partner who had one so scorned her. The more she thought about it, the more and more convinced Gina became that RJ had foolishly placed herself in serious danger, and to a point when she felt literally surrounded by warning bells.

Finally, her fears were unbearable. She'd at least make certain the officer probably assigned to guard RJ was alert. She got up and dressed, pocketed her cell phone, and strapped on her utility belt. The digital clock on the bedside table said 2:07 a.m. Should she call RJ? Yes, but wakening her wouldn't tell her if RJ was at home or someplace else. And if RJ was safe and secure in her own home, she'd risk real embarrassment over what an annoyed RJ would call childishness. She decided not to.

Out in the corridor, she saw the police officer assigned to guard her slouched in an upholstered chair, half asleep. She nudged him alert and got a "Sorry, Sergeant," as he struggled awake.

"It's okay," she said. "Can you text or call whomever was assigned to Detective Inspector Jones?"

The officer got out his cell phone, punched in numbers. He waited. Gina waited. After what seemed forever, he lowered the cell and said, "Guy's not responding."

Gina's reaction was instant. She said, "Get onto precinct central. Tell them I requested backup sent to 189 Barrow Street."

And before the startled officer could comply, Gina was down the carpeted corridor to the elevator.

Twenty-eight

❧

She drove fast, siren wailing unnecessarily through empty sleeping streets and into the poorer section of the suburbs. The houses were small and ordinary with barely a lawn separating each from the narrow tree-lined street that went by them. She turned off the siren several blocks short of Barrow, and when she got into RJ's block she costed, motor also off, to the curb not far from what she figured from the posted numbers on other homes to be number 189 and RJ's.

Getting out of the car, she silently walked down the street, barely lit by a lamp the far end, glad for her quiet running shoes and keeping to the deepest shadows just the same. Reaching what she figured had to be the right house, she saw no sign of light, and for a moment Gina thought once more that she was being stupidly foolish. God forbid RJ should find out she'd been there, hearing she had been perhaps from an awakened neighbor or because of some other reason. She'd try to stop the backup she'd foolishly asked for and got out her phone.

That's when she tripped and fell over the body of the uniformed police officer assigned to guard RJ. Rising, startled and for an instant not realizing what it was she'd fallen over, she felt her hands all sticky, knew it was blood, and quickly shone her phone light down to see the man dead and lying in a pool of his own blood by the camp chair in which he'd been sitting before a razor sharp knife, slashed with silent swiftness across his throat, had ended his life.

She quickly clicked off her light and held her breath, and then after what seemed only seconds, heard the unmistakable sound of a door opening and closing. Front door? Back door? It sounded like the one into the garage, and she'd hardly ducked behind the bushes separating the house from the neighboring one when two shadowy forms appeared coming out of the garage and carrying something long and bulky between them. Getting to a car parked in the street only a few feet beyond the house's driveway, they lifted the bundle up, rolled it into the trunk of the car, and got into the car themselves. Moments later, the car's motor came to life.

What happened then was all a blur to Gina: her

remembering RJ's once saying they took victims someplace before finishing them off, her negating her chances in immediately tackling two men, then moving so fast that weeks later everything was still unclear.

Simultaneously, as the car began to pull away from the curb, she reached her own police car she'd parked half a block away. Almost without thinking, she hit the ignition switch and jammed down on the accelerator. The police car leapt forward.

All her early years as a patrol officer took over, and she caught up to the car driven by one of the two men a block and a half away. Closing fast and without an instant of hesitation, she attacked just when the car had slowed and turned left into a side street, not following it around the corner herself but cutting across the corner regardless, crashing through a fence and then leaping over the grass lawn of the corner house, down onto the side street in time to smash into the fleeing car as it began to pick up speed again.

There was the violent shrieking metallic sound of the collision, then silence.

The crash left both cars wrecked, the engine front of the police car askew, the driver's door of the other car mangled and wrapped over the seat and the steering wheel, crushing the lifeless driver. The car's dazed passenger got out and started to stagger away into the darkness just as house lights began to turn on.

Gina was faster. Limping badly, and gasping

from shock, a wrenched knee, and broken ribs, she managed to free her Glock and trigger off a warning shot, and then caught up and leapt on the fleeing man, knocking him face down onto the street, herself on top him. Without thinking, Gina screamed, "Police! Don't move, don't move," and when the man's hands were firmly cuffed, she rose to find herself relieved of him by a police car arriving and two uniformed officers confronting her, ready to arrest until they realized she was a fellow cop.

With Gina frantically trying to explain, one got a wrecking bar to help her pry open the jammed-shut trunk of the smashed into car. Together they got out the woman they found in it and removed the duct tape from her eyes and mouth. RJ's face was battered and bloody but she could speak. Just. And she kept saying, "Gas, gas turned on. Gas. Mireille."

When Gina and one patrol officer got back to RJ's house, neighboring lights were beginning to turn on, and people were coming out and asking what was happening. Ignoring them, Gina got from the police car to the front door of 189, found it locked, and without an instant's hesitation, unholstered her Glock again and shot the lock out. Inside she fumbled and found a hallway light switch while the officer located the kitchen, where all four jets on the range were turned on.

And Gina found the still conscious woman on the hallway floor just as the officer got windows open and more lights on, and as the backup arrived on the block, three patrol cars, their blue and red roof lights flashing eerily, sirens moaning to silence.

Now barely able to keep moving, Gina ripped off duct tape wrapped around the dark-haired head and found herself looking at a heavily scarred face and eyes that stared back, one sightlessly. From the only word RJ had ever spoken about her private life, Gina knew at once who the woman was. She said, "It's okay, it's all okay. We've got your partner. She's safe."

Twenty-nine

The driver of the smashed-into getaway car carrying RJ was dead, but the police both in Covington and later in Chicago got enough evidence from the other man Gina had arrested, his naming names, and in a plea deal informing on nearly every aspect of the explosion that assured a closedown of the Chicago Six for at least a few years ahead.

Life in the second precinct CID of the Covington police returned to normal. Gina and RJ, the older detective out of hospital, her broken nose adding an additional slight distortion to her already plain boxer's face, together tackled minor arson in a violent domestic abuse case, an armed robbery of a jewelry store in which one of the store employees had been shot and a million dollars of jewelry seized, and a shooting in a pharmacy in which of the three left dead, one was the shooter.

They were their last cases together. RJ was given special dispensation to retire a year early. "I've got someone to look after who was pretty shook up by what happened," she told the reviewing board, which, given her extraordinary career, had no problem acquiescing to her request.

"Leaves me without a partner," Gina complained when she and others were having rounds at the Blue Light.

"Haley will find you someone," RJ said. "He did for me when I was stuck."

"Yeah, with instant love on both sides, if I remember right," came from Charlie Fargo amidst laughter.

"Want to be a fucking cop, that's the way it goes," Ace added.

"Amen," RJ said.

When everyone had had enough and started, one by one, to peel off for home, RJ said to Gina, "Favor, maybe?"

"Anything. What?"

"Well ..." RJ looked unusually unsure of herself before continuing, but going ahead anyway with a strangely shy smile. "Mireille loves classical music, and when I told her that you sometimes played the violin professionally, she asked if you couldn't possibly come over some night and play." She added quickly, "She's a great cook."

Gina didn't hesitate. "Sure," she said. "Why not?"

They arranged a Saturday night, and when it came and Gina went first from the office to her apartment to dump her police gear and get her violin, she stopped before turning out the lights to ritually glance over the small framed photographs lining the top of the dresser.

The day before she'd added a new one. It was a painting on one side of a canvas. Gina had framed it and had it cleaned, so that now one could clearly see the book an old woman was reading as well as the bonnet on her head. The CID office staff had secured it from being shut away in the case-closed section of the archives and had given it to her as a reward for the work she'd done on the explosive homicide that the police chief and commissioner didn't seem to think much of since they barely mentioned either her or the painting in their official reports.

"Just to remember one case in your work as a police detective," RJ had said.

About the Author

David Osborn, for over sixty years a writer, lives in Connecticut with his wife, a once American and European ballerina, then renowned in international health policy. Their daughter, a PhD psychologist, practices in Sydney, Australia. Their lawyer son is an advocate for the welfare of animals worldwide.

Also by David Osborn

NOVELS

The Glass Tower
Open Season
The French Decision
Heads
Love and Treason
Murder on Martha's Vineyard
The Last Pope
Murder on the Chesapeake
Murder in the Napa Valley
The Cape Cod Blue
The Head Hunters
Delta Red
Alicia's Secret
A Cold Wind from the Andes
Looking Back (a memoir)
Eventide
The Somersville Bodies
Cold Case 369

FOR CHILDREN

Jessica and the Crocodile Knight (a novel)
The eight-book *Jessica* series (novellas)
Ophelia and Her Forest Friends (series of ten stories)

FILMS (STORY AND SCREENPLAY)

Chase a Crooked Shadow – Warner Bros.
Malaga – Warner Bros.
Deadlier Than the Male – J. Arthur Rank
Some Girls Do – J. Arthur Rank
Maroc 7 – J. Arthur Rank
Follow the Boys – MGM
The Trap – Columbia (Academy Award nominee for
    Best Foreign Film)
Penny Gold – J. Arthur Rank

Murder, She Said – MGM

Open Season – Columbia

Whoever Slew Auntie Roo? – Paramount & American International

Beat Girl – Associated British

The Road to Dusty Death – J. Arthur Rank

The Games – Associated British

Les Petits Rats – Disney (production begun, then canceled)

Eagle at Sundown – Dragon Films (in production when canceled)

Winter Holiday – MGM (production canceled before scripting)

Hunters' Horn – McCahon Productions (production canceled; finance failure)

HMS Ulysses – Rank (production halted when a key warship was unavailable)

Peking to Paris – Volpi Productions (production canceled in favor of documentary production; see below)

FEATURE-LENGTH DOCUMENTARIES

Fangio, The History of Formula One Racing – Volpi Productions

Why Ireland – Irish Tourist Bureau

TELEVISION (THREE-ACT PLAYS AND SERIES)

Why George Brown Hanged (BTPA nominee for Best Three-act Play)

Three on a Gas Ring (BTPA nominee for Best Three-act Play)

Bouquet for Miss Olive (BTPA nominee for Best Three-act Play)

Arthur of the Britons (BSWA award winner for Best British Children's Series)

The Antiquers (Irish sitcom; story, pilot, and six episodes in the series)